The Wolves Came Down from the Mountain

Michael Strong

THE WOLVES
CAME DOWN FROM
THE MOUNTAIN

WALKER AND COMPANY
NEW YORK

First published in the United States of America
in 1979 by the Walker Publishing Company, Inc.

ISBN: 0-8027-5414-7

Library of Congress Catalog Card Number: 79-65164

Printed in the United States of America

10 9 8 7 6 5 4 3 2 1

To Jean, Jem, Caroline, Margrietha and Jane

Prologue

The machine pistol was becoming an abomination. Karl Ploner eased himself ten millimetres in the nest he had made for himself. His nerve endings first quivered then relaxed as he gained another brief moment of relief. Twenty-two hours! Twenty-two bone-aching, muscle-cramping, blood-chilling hours of waiting that brought the metabolism to the edge of catalepsey. He would count two hundred, very slowly at sluggish pulse rate – then he would reach down beside him and pull up the flask. He knew to a millilitre how much coffee was left. There were exactly four swallows and he would take two of them. It couldn't be long now. The briefing in the police station had been explicit. The school bus would leave the church hall at eight o'clock and would reach the ambush point near the woods a quarter of an hour later. There the terrorists would be waiting for them, waiting to take them and hold them – forty school kids – while the demands were made and while the whole world watched in fascinated titillation. Except that it wasn't going to be like that. Not with him, Polizei Sergeant Karl Ploner, seven years' service in the West German police and first-class marksman and the rest of his friends already in position in a counter-ambush almost a whole day before the terrorist group had arrived. That tip-off must have been a real prize. They'd admitted as much at the briefing.

He twisted his wrist – eight o'clock on a cold October night. The kids would be on their way now.

You had to give it to the terrorists; they were marvellous. They couldn't be more than a hundred metres away, and yet he'd heard nothing. They must have been as silent as a pack of wolves running mute before the leader gives tongue. He started to flex his fingers and checked again that the safety catch was off. Far away he heard the first murmur of an engine as the school bus changed gear, coming round the bend that would bring it down from the hillside. Karl Ploner moistened his lips and took comfort from the knowledge that he was not alone. Within a radius of two kilometres there were close on a thousand armed police and troops – the attack group, the close-support group, the services section and then, at two kilometres' distance, the road blocks, the platoons of footsloggers – all ready to fan out and start patiently searching if any of them got away. The bus was getting nearer.

The driver of the school bus felt the sweat collecting for several seconds before it trickled down the back of his spine. He was almost there. 'Laminated glass,' they had said – 'would stop anything.' But supposing they were using Armalites. 'Go through anything,' they said. So there you were! What was it they said? 'Irresistible force meets immovable object.' Anyway, all the kids were back at the church hall with their teachers wondering what the hell was going on, while he and his mates were out looking for the big bad wolves.

The glass at the side window starred and he felt the wicked impact of the terrorist bullet, then the windscreen was an opaque mass of whiteness as he turned the wheel, slewing across the road so they would have to come at him up or down the tarmac and give the waiting police a clear field of fire. The plaster dummies at the windows bounced and joggled as he jabbed his

8

finger at the button and started off the taped screams. The night opened up as he dropped to the floor where the armour plating would protect him and he covered his ears with his hands to still the fear inside him. There was no one to see and no one to tell.

Karl Ploner was standing, body crouched as he fired the second clip. Five-round bursts traversing the ground in front of the bus, plastering the terrorist position. He could see the winking lights as other police began to fire from the far side of the road and he gave a sigh of relief as the first flare arced up from the wood followed by a second and a third. Then the searchlights were on and he could see the bastards. He snatched at the extendable shoulder-piece, pulling it out, clipping it into place and jerked the weapon into his armpit. Now there could be some real shooting.

The terrorists were in a state of shock. The noise was deafening and they fired blindly into the night, confused by the flares. Their leader, sick at heart, pulled out a grenade – one of the ten that were to have held the world entranced as they bargained for the lives of the children. He pulled the pin. There was little hope now but they would show their successors how to die. He gave a convulsive heave, lifting his body from the road as he hurled the missile at the bus. It dropped a metre short and bounced once before it disappeared under the vehicle for a whole second and a half before erupting into orange and red flame. Forty dead children. It would be worth it. Then a horrible anxiety filled his mind. Suppose – suppose! A bullet at two thousand four hundred feet per second put an end to his thinking.

．　　．　　．　　．　　．

In Geneva a thermostat reached its final point of expansion before cutting in, blowing cold air across the neck of the fleshy, hooked-nosed man sitting back in the high, padded, black swivel chair. He felt his skin contract as he heard the message.

'You mean the police were there, waiting for them?'

He listened and his voice rose in incredulity.

'You mean there's nothing left?'

Another pause – then a hardening of the voice.

'All right. They seem to have won. There must be complete disengagement. No! There must be no retaliation! Just leave it – *leave* it! No! You will *not*! You will leave things exactly as they are. You will *NOT* compound disaster.'

He put the phone down and stared at the far wall. For ten minutes there was no movement until he reached forward and pressed a switch on the panel in the centre of his desk. The woman who answered his call was in her mid-forties – she wore a tailored suit with the skirt a centimetre longer than most of her age group would accept as the norm. She stood silently.

'Bring me the *curricula vitae* of all the lower council members, will you please, Inge?'

The erudition escaped her but she grasped the stems of the words and turned to go back to her filing cabinets. Inge Ludwig was an empress among secretaries and there was little that would cause her to question a command. She brought an armful of papers.

'They are all here, Herr Fafner – all except Mr Harrod's. You have that already.'

For an hour the heavily built man stared at the files, turning the pages with a thick finger. Every few minutes he lit a cigar. They were made in Havana and calculated with exquisite precision to bring tears of perfection to a smoker's eyes. Two minutes later he would stub out the remaining thirteen centimetres and wait a whole fifty seconds before lighting another as he flicked over the pages, staring at them with eyes red-rimmed with emotion.

It was the first time he had had to face the certainty that his organization had been penetrated. It had to be an infiltration – the penalties were so horrendous that no true member would have broken security – it had to be an outsider. Something would have to be done and it would have to be done from here. He would have to bypass the councils – both of them – and make it a headquarters operation. He sat back in his chair and thought for several minutes before leaning forward to press the button again. This time he asked for the previous month's intelligence summary for Alpine France. He had remembered something that might be useful.

I

The French Alps are dominated by Mont Blanc. There is nothing nearby that can approach it. The Giant's Teeth are a good eight hundred metres lower and eight hundred metres is nearly two and a half thousand feet. In winter the whole is an eye-searing, soft-footed, icicle-tinkling world of sun-sparkled whiteness, broken only by the green-grey points of the needles – the Aiguille Verte, the Aiguille Drue, the Aiguille du Midi – standing up dark with pointed tips and sides too steep for the snow to settle.

There are major valleys and minor valleys and the minor valleys have yet smaller valleys, wandering sideways and upwards, mere fissures scratching into the mountains, narrowing rapidly as they rise until they end as a crack in the rock face, full of shrubs and coarse mountain grass, drinking the summer streams that come down from the edge of the perennial snow.

Chamonix is the great centre for Mont Blanc but there are other places, towns as well as villages that stretch in a chain, linked by the major roads, towards the lakes of Switzerland. The people who live there are like their mountains, more grey, more reserved, more rock-like than Frenchmen on the plains.

In winter and in summer everywhere is crowded with skiers, climbers, walkers, or the slightly fat and breathless taking gentle exercise or attending the tennis and golf clinics that offer them the excuse to go into high places.

In spring and autumn the French are virtually alone; their visitors, who provide them with their living, are back in the cities, earning the wealth and acquiring the pallor that will both be dissipated in the next season. October is the most desolate month when even the students, taking the cheap low-season bargains, have gone and the first snows are only beginning to threaten.

It is then that the mountain men prepare for their winter, stacking the cut wood against the side of the house, where the eaves will shelter it from the snows and the warmth from the stove, seeping through the wall, will dry and twist the timber ready for burning.

Occasionally, there will be the out-of-season traveller, the writer seeking a place where the air is clean and where the hours crouched over a table can be relieved by hard exercise from the moment he sets foot beyond the door, or lovers meeting in guilty seclusion, when the warmth of their bodies adds delicious luxury in contrast with the dampness and cold outside.

·　·　·　·　·

In one of the higher Alpine valleys Pierre Pecheur swung the double-handed axe and split a log almost in two with a precision learnt over more than fifty years. The soft thump as the axe-edge met the chopping-block sent a gentle echo up the side of the mountain. With the certainty of age he bent, fingering the wood, selecting the next plump-ringed victim. He set up the piece and had begun his swing before he saw the first of the shadows. He tried to turn but the weight of the axe was against him, carrying his arms down with it. Before he could lift his only weapon out of the gripping lips of the tree-stump, arms were about him, hands prising at his fingers. There was time for one last glimpse of the mountain tops, brilliant white against the sky, before the axe head struck through his cheek-bones and, a second and a half later, before even his body had reached the ground he was dead and the first powdering of early snow began to settle on his body.

His attackers turned to look anxiously at the house, but the woman who stood staring from the window was wrapped in her thoughts and had seen nothing.

She pressed her forehead against the coldness of the window-pane, watching her breath misting the glass and the snowflakes brushing past. It would be soon now. He should be here before dark and then . . . She thought of the last time and felt the spasm that started down in her loins, peaking to intensity as she remembered the things they had done; how it had gone on and on until she thought it would never stop. She had to think of something counter-erotic, something that would bring her fever heat down to a tolerable level. She thought of her husband.

The divorce had been made final three months before but she was still unused to the feeling of freedom. She felt her passions cooling as she went over the sterile nights in her mind. To think she had saved herself for *that*. Five years of frustration and torment while the first horror turned to questioning wonder, soon replaced by loathing and complete withdrawal until the final ugly parting with all its glare of publicity.

She moved her forehead from side to side and hugged her body with her arms. It was all different now — discovering love, or was it lust, at twenty-eight and taking to it like a harlot of ancient times. Even the name she had taken to conceal her identity was culled from antiquity; Juliette Montague; she smiled at the joke.

Here she was, high in the French Alps, alone and waiting.

There was something plucking at the edge of her consciousness. She tried to think, frowning in concentration. It was something negative. Then she had it: it was old Pierre – he wasn't chopping wood any more. She heard the footsteps on the stairs. Probably it was a message. She felt a coldness on her skin. Perhaps he wouldn't be coming – or he would be late or . . . Perhaps it was James himself, two hours before his time.

There was no knock. The door opened and a man stepped into the room. He could be no more than thirty but there were deep clefts down his cheeks and his brown hair had a grey tinge at the temples. He was wearing a fawn leather jacket, expensively flared into a long hip-length skirt. Whipcord trousers were tucked into padded walking boots. He stood just inside the door.

Juliette stared at him, uncomprehending. Then she felt the chill of the room as he moved two paces towards her. Behind him came a barrel of a man – thick dark hair and the tight denim jacket and jeans of a Neapolitan procureur. Behind him again was a thin wisp of a desiccated human male with cold blue eyes that stared at her from under white eyebrows. Juliette reached backwards and pressed her hands against the window-sill, watching the smile broaden on the leader's face.

'Mme Montague?'

She felt a surge of hope. They knew her by her assumed name, so it must be all right. It was probably something about . . . His smile stretched wide now, white teeth showing.

'I'm afraid we're going to take you away, Juliette. You'll come with us and not make a fuss because . . .'

He saw the beginnings of the scream and leaped forward, wrapping an arm round her, pulling her helplessly against him as he got his hand over her mouth. She could feel the coldness of the leather against her hands and smelt the faint garlic odour on his breath.

'Now, Juliette! You're going to be good, aren't you?'

The others had moved round behind her and she could feel their hands pulling and lifting her clothing. She squirmed against them as she felt the cold air on her legs and fingers against her skin.

'Now be still, my girl, or you will have a broken needle in your backside. *Hold still!*'

She felt the jab and the swelling tension as the injection was pressed into her body, then the swift jerk as the hypodermic was withdrawn.

'You can start counting if you like, my dear. It will act very quickly.'

She could feel nothing except the arms that were holding her, crushing her body. Then came the rushing blackness and the bare seconds' warning before she became unconscious.

.   .   .   .   .

The snow was turning from a light powdering to a full-flaked shower and James Rigbey had to use the wipers as he turned off the main road up from Champbiére into the final valley. He checked his watch. Four o'clock; he had said five. He wondered if she would give him time for a shower or if she would be at him as soon as he got through the door. He smiled and shook his head ruefully. What a way to spend a week's leave! Shacked up with a woman who'd been in all the papers a few months before, teaching her what it was all about. He thought of the dark hair, with its copper tints, deliberately hanging loose — brushed a hundred times in the evening, so that she could dispense with hairdressers — the high cheek-bones, the mouth with just a hint of pushing teeth that sent the lips into the beginning of a kiss. He changed gear for the final climb. The roof was showing now. He let his mind drift to her body as he pulled off the track in front of old Pierre's house.

There had been a heavy-tyred vehicle there before him and he stared at the pressed mud as he got out of his car. He opened the back door and leaned inside, gathering up the bottle of cognac and the fresh loaves. He would take them round to the kitchen for Pierre then climb the backstairs. She liked it that way — the footsteps on the stairs, the brief knock on the door and then . . . He shook his head again. Ah! Yes! And then!

He saw the blood first. It had run in a long trickle from Pierre's head and the snow had soaked it up leaving the bright streak startlingly red against its whiteness. Slowly Rigbey crouched and put the loaves on the ground. He held the bottle by its neck as he approached the woodpile. He stared for a long moment at Pierre's body then turned and ran hard round the side of the house to his car. It was not the panic run of a man in terror but an athlete's sprint, covering the ground hard and fast.

He swung open the driving door, slid behind the wheel and started the engine. There was room to turn and he accelerated fast, scattering slush and gravel as he drove back down the track. After three hundred metres he stopped and manoeuvred the car until it was facing back uphill. He got out, opened the rear door and felt delicately under the arm-rest. He prised loose the retaining studs then lifted the padded leather and took out the short barrelled revolver and the pack of twelve spare cartridges. It was not his combat weapon and it was useless out of doors but at five yards it was a great comfort. He broke it open, checked the rounds and tested the spin of the cylinder before snapping it together. He laid it on the front seat beside him and drove slowly back to the house.

He pulled up outside the front door and was out of the car and into the house in one fast movement. In the hall he stood, arm outstretched and gun pointed, searching for danger. There was no sound and he moved to the living-room door, turning the knob slowly before going through fast, dropping to one knee. Pierre's cat leaped for the piano from its rug by the stove and crouched, spitting at him in its fright.

He searched the house and there was nothing. There was supper laid out on the kitchen table and Juliette's bedroom showed no signs of an attack. He stood and stared at the bed.

There was the faint sound of a heavy engine and Rigbey crossed to the window. A four-wheel-drive, white-painted vehicle was crawling down the second-ary road from the upper valley, lurching over the ruts. There were no passengers – just the driver, a light fawn shape behind the wheel.

Rigbey ran down the stairs and into the living room, where the net curtains gave him concealment. The car drew in before the house and he watched the driver climb out, looking cautiously round him with his lined face showing his anxiety as he inspected Rigbey's car. Rigbey moved to the door and stepped into the open, holding his revolver behind him. The man swung round, startled, then relaxed.

'Mr Rigbey, how nice to see you so early. We weren't expecting you for another hour.'

There was fear behind the eyes and the bland voice had a ragged edge to it as though the breath ran out just before the end of a sentence.

Rigbey moved forward a couple of steps to bring himself into certain range.

'Where's Juliette?'

'Ah! Mr Rigbey – Mme Montague.' He gave a deprecating downward flapping gesture with his hand. 'You see, Mr Rigbey, it is my superiors who wish to speak to you about Mme Montague. I have just come to collect the body.'

He paused, looking at Rigbey uncertainly. 'You did know about the body – didn't you? Or have I made a terrible mistake?'

'I know about Pierre Pecheur. He's dead – behind the woodpile. Is there another one?'

The man in the fawn leather coat wasn't listening, he was staring over Rigbey's shoulder at the track that led down the valley.

'Ah! here they come, Mr Rigbey. Now you will be able to ask all the questions you wish. Would you mind if I went and tidied up at the back?'

'Stay where you are!'

Rigbey moved to his left to get the man between him and the approaching car. It was a Mercedes and it was riding smoothly over the rough road.

'What's your name?'

'I'm Videl.'

'Just keep standing there, Videl, and hope you're

precious enough to make your boss keep in line, otherwise you'll be minus a kneecap.'

'Mr Rigbey. I assure you. You have nothing to fear from me or my superiors. You will find them in a most co-operative frame of mind.'

The Mercedes pulled up a cautious twenty metres away and the driver and his passenger got out slowly and walked towards the house holding their arms at an angle to their bodies, flat palmed, hands turned slightly outwards.

They were both Teutonic. Short blond hair, blue-grey eyes – tall and bulky. They were expensively dressed and dark worsted trousers above town shoes showed beneath their heavy navy overcoats. The driver spoke.

'Mr Rigbey, my companion and I are unarmed and Videl will throw down his gun, while he has his back to you.' He turned his eyes to Videl, who reached slowly, cross-handed, into his leather coat and brought out a heavy Browning automatic between fingers and thumb. He dropped it in the snow and kicked it to one side.

'Well done, Videl. Now, Mr Rigbey, my name is Streicher, you do not need to know my companion's name. May we go into the house and talk before the stove? It is a little cold out here – is it not? We wil precede you, of course.'

Rigbey nodded. They moved into the house and intc the living room. Streicher slapped his hands in front of the stove.

'Mr Rigbey, we know who you are. James Rigbey is your real name and you are the front man for British Security. You are the man out in the open with whom contact can always be made. You are the negotiator of their bargains and the messenger of your chiefs. At present you are having a clandestine affaire with a lady who has taken the name of Juliette Montague to avoid the publicity that came from her fairly recent and highly sordid divorce from one of your prominent and, until a few months ago, most popular public figures. Your affaire may or may not be known to your superiors. It is an entirely personal matter and conducted only during your off-duty time and leaves. You were anticipating, no doubt, an energetic and exhausting week in this remote spot.'

Streicher paused enquiringly, with his head on one side. Rigbey stared at him and said nothing. The German smiled.

'Very wise, Mr Rigbey. No admissions, of course. I will continue.' He stared at the stove for a moment.

'Mr Rigbey, you have heard of the Wolves?'

He looked sharply into James's face as he spoke, pausing a moment and nodding.

'Very good indeed, Mr Rigbey. Not a flicker of emotion. I will not elaborate, in case you really have not heard of us. Just let me say that the Wolves have returned and are abroad once more in Europe and they are seizing the lambs wherever they can find them. Unfortunately, we have been penetrated by one of your people, Mr Rigbey.' He smiled and brushed away a non-existent protest. 'No, no, not necessarily from your organization but from *someone*'s security. This means that we cannot hunt with the confidence of the past few years and we are greatly distressed by this.' He smiled again, 'You see! I am being quite frank with you.' He got up and stood with his back to the stove.

'Mr Rigbey, we have taken Juliette Montague as a hostage. She is presently on her way to a safe place. We will not announce her capture and we would ask

22

you to return immediately to your employers. You will present them with our demand that they, or their Continental colleagues, will remove the man they have infiltrated into our council, whereupon we will release Mme Montague. If you do not we will broadcast the fact that we are holding her prisoner and that she had taken you for her lover. There will be other threats, of course. You can imagine the sensation, Mr Rigbey. What a spot you will be in. We will, of course, require proof that the man who is suddenly missing from our council was, in fact, the infiltrator, so I'm afraid it will do little good to eliminate one of our members at random. You will correspond with us by advertisement in the *International Herald Tribune*. Just say "contact finished" and sign it "Rigbey".'

For the first time Rigbey spoke.

'Supposing this is true and we agree. What will happen to our man?'

'My dear Mr Rigbey. He will go free, of course. We are not witch-hunting. We do not want him delivered up for vengeance. We simply wish to be rid of him. Then you must start all over again. We expect that and will not hold a grudge against you.'

The German's teeth were milk white and showed like gravestones as he smiled.

Rigbey raised his revolver. 'It won't be like that, Streicher. I shall take you to the French Security – just you – and then we'll see how much you can tell us.'

Streicher sighed gently. He shrugged.

'Very well, Mr Rigbey. Shall we go? You will find us quite innocuous, I fear.'

They moved towards the door. Rigbey tensed. This would be the danger spot. They would have to go out first and they could fan, left and right, as soon as they

23

were outside. Streicher half lifted his hands as he went through the door. The other two followed calmly. Rigbey relaxed. It was too late for them to try anything now. He stepped out into the snow.

An arm went round his neck and a knee drove into his back, grinding deep into his spine. A hand caught his wrist, pulling it up into the air and he had a glimpse of Streicher and the other two diving for the ground. Then he was head first in the snow looking up at the young blond athlete who had thrown him down.

The blond youth picked up Rigbey's gun.

'Get up slowly, mister.'

Rigbey obeyed and the atmosphere relaxed. Streicher was brushing the snow off his clothes. He had never stopped smiling.

'So there you are, Mr Rigbey! We kept one of our party back as a reserve – he was on the floor of the car. You now have a week. Today is Friday. We allow you until a week tomorrow. I'm afraid I can't promise that your Juliette will not be harmed – that is certainly not part of the bargain. But she won't be killed. Move quickly, Mr Rigbey. She will be very uncomfortable and she will be crying your name many times in the next few days.'

2

Juliette Montague was not far away. She was being held in a hut that was occupied only during summer when the cattle were brought up to the high pasture. It was at the head of a tiny tributary valley that probed into the mountainside less than four kilometres from Pierre

24

Pecheur's house. There were two rooms – a large living room and a smaller bedroom. There was an earth privy in a lean-to, which was reached through a back door. Spring water filled a cistern, then ran on down the valley in a small stream. Juliette Montague sat on a wooden chair in the living room and stared at the two men. The drug had worn off, leaving her thick-tongued and sickly. She could feel her drawn cheeks and sensed the whiteness of her face. The men were sitting in canvas camp chairs, the older one reading a newspaper, while the fat one was looking at an Italian porno-graphic magazine, flicking over the pages with intense fingers. She could see the entwined bodies on the front cover and could hear the man breathing through wet parted lips. There were three more chairs and a table in the room and an old paraffin cooking stove in one corner. Three bedding rolls lay in a pile by the wall and there were two cardboard boxes of groceries under the table. A cast-iron woodstove heated the shack.

She had been to the privy once to be sick. The thin man had stayed outside the door while the stench of urine and excreta had made her vomit her heart out There was no way of escape at the back. Within a few metres the rock face began to rise, hemming the hut in on three sides. The windows of the hut were tightly shut and there was no sound of the car until a door slammed, then the man in the fawn leather jacket stepped into the room.

Videl had come through the door quietly and he saw the startled fear on the faces of the two men. The girl was slumped back in a wooden chair, her face yellow-grey, arms hanging limply down towards the floor. He noted her clothes – cream woollen roll-necked sweater, dark green woollen skirt and under it thick, knitted oatmeal tights. The clothes weren't too bad for what they wanted. He wondered if she would fight or if the spirit would go. She moved her hand slightly and his eyes caught the perfect manicure of her nails and the flashing diamonds. No, she wouldn't fight. Take this sort out of their secure, moneyed environment and they collapsed. Look what she'd taken from that sod of a husband of hers. He looked at the men's questioning faces and reassured them.

'All's well!'

He turned back to the woman.

'My name is Videl – spelt V-I-D-E-L, pronounced Vee-dell. The older gentleman is Vosper and the fat one is Beppo. They have other names but that is all you need to know. You will be in our charge for one week if things go well and two or more weeks if things go badly. We have no instructions to be gentle with you, only to keep you alive, so your treatment depends entirely on yourself.'

His voice was flat, matter-of-fact. There was no emotion, no over-emphasis, just a statement. He moved across the room until he was standing over her. There had been no change in her expression, just the wide-eyed stare. Could she just be dumb or was she too shocked to take things in? Better put some life in her.

Once again he spoke evenly and without aggression.

'You will now go into the bedroom and remove your shoes and tights.'

That got through to her. Her eyes widened even further. They were brown shading to gold. She opened her mouth and tried to speak but swallowed convulsively with a bob of the chin before she could get the word out.

'Why?'

He gave no warning movement, just brought his hand up in a sweeping arc from his side, smashing the fingers obliquely upwards against her cheek, following through as she jerked away. The chair overturned and she fell backwards, hitting the floor hard with her shoulder, her legs straddled in a waving jumble of rucked skirt and exposed thighs.

Juliette stared up at Videl from the floor. The pain in her cheek was swelling into puffed agony and, as she lifted herself up off the boards with one hand, she put the other to the welts that were forming on her skin. He stood over her, legs apart, hands on his hips. The creases had deepened in the sides of his face and the light brown hair had shaken forward over his forehead.

'You will never . . . *never*, question anything you are told to do. You will do exactly as you are told. Now go.'

He stood back and watched her as she pushed herself painfully to her feet. She staggered slightly and caught the back of a chair to steady herself. The pain in her cheek had reached its limit now and she walked slowly to the bedroom. She closed the door behind her.

There was an iron single bedstead with an old hair mattress and three blankets in a pile. Apart from that there was one wooden chair and a stained table with a porcelain bowl. The windows were barred.

She sat down on the edge of the bed and eased off her shoes then pulled up her skirt and hooked her thumbs in the waistband of her tights. She pulled them down over her hips on to her thighs then sat on the bed and lifted each leg in turn as she pulled at the woollen material. She lowered her legs hurriedly as Videl pushed into the room. He was carrying a short length of stainless steel chain. At each end there was an open brace-

27

let, perhaps two inches broad. They made a musical tinkling as they swung in his hand. He smiled approvingly.

'Beppo is sulking because I won't let him help me. But there is no need, is there?'

He raised his eyebrows. She stared at the blueness of his eyes and felt her stomach contract into a hard knot.

She gripped hard at the edge of the mattress. She could feel the tears on her cheek. She looked at the swinging steel.

'What are those for?'

The teeth showed a millimetre between his lips. 'Believe me, Juliette, these are for your comfort. We are ten kilometres from the nearest house and the snow is settling outside. Without your shoes and with these round your ankles – why, you can move freely round the house. We won't have to watch you every minute – no quick dashes for freedom and, if you did get away – why, how easy to bring you back!'

He moved towards her, pulling the chain out to its full length. It was eighteen inches long.

'Lie on the bed!'

She pushed herself back, crouching stiff-armed, kneeling, legs to one side. She shook her head disbelievingly. 'No . . . No!'

Videl turned his head and called.

'Beppo – I will need you after all.'

The fat Italian padded into the room. His mouth was open, bottom lip glistening red and brown stained teeth showed as he reached out to hold her, dragging her back as she tried to shuffle across the bed. Half sitting, half lying across her hips, he pinioned her thighs with his body as he held her wrists.

The girl screamed, short screams of hysteria as Videl

pressed the bracelets round her ankles. One end of each was perforated with a selection of three slots, which he strained over the staple of the other end. He tested the fit by sliding the anklets up her calves and pressed them down to her heels before taking two small padlocks from his pocket and snapping them through the staples. He stood up and nodded to Beppo.

'Let her go!'

The girl was twisting her head from side to side, grinding her face into the coarse mattress. She had stopped screaming and was crying with sharp whistling intakes of breath, her hands clenched as she writhed on the bed.

Videl smiled. It was perfect. It was amazing. He'd had his doubts but the lecturers had been completely and exactly right. His voice showed none of his satisfaction.

'You are now free to move about. Come and join us when you feel better.'

. . . . . .

In London, just off St James's Street, round the back of the square, the recriminations were made sharper by the fear of men whose careers depend on their secrecy and who see exposure becoming alarmingly possible.

The Director of Security would have been less unnerved if it hadn't been for Mealie Jimmy. He was a retired northern Chief Constable, who had been given a consultancy, with the Yard, on terrorist activities. He was sitting biding his time.

The director's nervousness showed in the short staccato barks.

'We *know* it's bad. We *know* what the consequences will be. We *know* what the Prime Minister will say to a security scandal. But let us wait until Rigbey gets back here. We only have the phone report to go on.'

Mealie Jimmy began to rumble, then coughed, clearing his throat aggressively before speaking.

'But do we know who the infiltrator *is* and why the hell haven't we heard of the Wolves before? I've checked with our lot and we've hardly anything on them at all.'

The director tried obvious patience.

'Because we know very little ourselves and because, so far as we know, they don't operate over here. They're Continental and they've never given us trouble. We get routine reports from our friends over there but Rigbey is picking up Glasiére in Paris and bringing him over in the plane.' He looked at his watch. 'They should have been here by now.'

The consultant sucked his teeth with a wet smacking sound.

'And what bargaining power do you have, to save us from a security scandal?' He broke off and rolled his eyes to the ceiling. '. . . Think of it, British spy, sleeping around with a famous divorcee, ex-wife of . . . Bloody hell – *think* of it – now held hostage. The television will *eat* this one. It has every bloody thing – sex, mystery – and a security service looking as foolish as . . .' He stopped again and gave an upward shrug of the shoulders with outstretched palms that made the director squirm in his chair. 'Anyway, suppose it *is* the French who have got a man into the Wolves' lair, how can you persuade them to drop him?'

The director was embarrassed and looked across at the tall lean balding man, who had sat silent, slightly drawn back from the half circle of armchairs.

'What do you think, Jones?'

The tall man's face remained impassive. He shifted slightly in his chair and the expensive cloth of his suit caught the light.

'We can bargain, sir. We have plenty on the Middle East we could give them and the use of our facilities — they're better than the French will ever have. Oh! yes, we could bargain all right. But could I say that would not be enough . . .'

'No you can't, Jones. It will have to be enough. Let's meet that one when it comes.' The director was terse. Another minute and Jones would have been blabbing their contingency plan that had been adapted in the last two hours from one of the many that were locked away in filing cabinets in the basement. The director disagreed with Jones about how much you should let others know. Hell's teeth — how much did the CIA let out to *their* masters?

There was a tap at the door and Rigbey came in followed by a smiling dark-haired man in a navy overcoat. He was Glasiére and their liaison in Paris. For half an hour Rigbey filled in the background. Then the director put the question.

'Well, Glasiére. *Have* you got a man in there and will you drop him? Our gratitude will be enormous!'

Glasiére smiled and pulled a slim gold-cornered notebook from his pocket.

'M. le Directeur, you will understand that this must be ratified by our highest authorities but we will co-operate with you on the following conditions.'

He began to read from his list. Item one, item two, item three. By the time he had got to item seven the director was beginning to make exasperated noises and sighed gustily as Glasiére finished at number eight.

'So that's *all* you want.'

'It has to be ratified, of course, M. le Directeur.'

The director looked at Jones then at Mealie Jimmy. Mealie Jimmy spoke.

'Bloody hell, Glasiére, you don't want much, do you!' He looked for confirmation at the director who was staring at his fingernails. The director lifted his head.

'We have a week, don't we? Well, we will just have to see how government reacts to this proposal.' His face showed his distaste. 'We will have to take it at cabinet level.'

Rigbey looked sharply at the director. He could feel the bile rising inside him. He thought of her body – then her face. He moved his shoulders inside his jacket, feeling the muscles tightening. Grey eyes stared out of the broad face, the massive frame deceptively concealed in its London suiting tense and uncompromising. He kept his voice deliberately neutral.

'They did make a point of it that the girl wasn't going to be exactly comfortable during this week.'

Mealie Jimmy stared at him coldly. His voice was venomous.

'What the hell has that got to do with it?'

3

Mealie Jimmy had left them to it and the director, Glasiére, Rigbey and Jones were getting down to business. There had been only one outburst of petulance from the director and he was now trying to make amends, listening carefully without interrupting.

'Give it us again, Glasiére.'

The Frenchman smiled the cat-creamed smile of the man who is watching others in trouble and who is going to bring off a highly beneficial coup for his country.

'M. le Directeur, it is true. We have a man in the lower council of the Wolves.' He made a deprecating gesture as only the French can. 'While this is an achievement and allowed us to alert the Germans about the school-bus ambush, it is not, unfortunately, enough. They use the cell system. There are cells in many European countries – several cells in some of them. Each cell has a member of the lower council. It is they who make the tactical policy decisions. It is with them that a client will negotiate. They do not, however, know any details about cells other than their own, nor do they know which cells are which. Above them is a higher council and, we suspect, a top man, who is never seen.'

'And their objects?'

'We do not know – we know only that they will organize any form of violence and are very good at it. The lower council assesses the viability of any application that comes in. It goes to the higher council for approval and then down to a cell for action. The leader of each cell has a code name and the higher council selects which shall do the operation. One cell sets up the operation but 'it is always carried out by a cell from another country. In, out, on guard – as we once said in the army.'

The director was hesitant.

'And you will really withdraw your man if we pay your price?'

Glasiére nodded. He looked down at his hands,

spreading the fingers out, one by one, making sure they were still there.

'Most certainly, sir, we have considered, very carefully, the advantages to be gained and we will be quite content with our bargain. Please understand, though, we have to get our man out safely and we may not be able to wait for the whole week. We will, however, warn you if we have to reduce the time, so please let us know as soon as possible if you accept.'

Glasiére left shortly afterwards, leaving the director uneasy and suspicious. He turned to the other two.

'What's made the French so bloody co-operative? Even though they're asking for the earth I wouldn't have given up an infiltrator in a position like that.'

Jones was staring at the ceiling. He too was wondering.

Their suspicion was justified. Glasiére had told them the truth but not the whole truth. He had not mentioned the second infiltrator working her way upwards in the Wolves organization who had, only the previous week, been nominated to a place on the lower council. There had been the death of the previous cell leader in an underground explosion that had wrecked half a row of houses on the outskirts of Nice and now the local star was rising fast indeed. She was the darling of French security, walking with her dancer's walk, through dangers that caused the old ones, the men who had survived, to sweat with fear on her behalf, caused the controllers who now sat at desks to recall their own days in the field and made even the agnostics pray for her. She was only twenty-two and they wondered how long she would live.

The director and Jones looked at each other. Jones

waited for his superior to speak. It was his privilege to take the lead.

'So, what are we going to do, Jones?'

'We have a week, sir. We'll ask for co-operation from all friendly countries, of course.'

'Of course. But that won't include the French. We've got a week! Is there anything else? We've already discussed the strike group.'

'No, sir. We can't rely on the cabinet agreeing to the French terms and, if they don't, we are in it up to our eyes. We *must* mount an operation to get to the girl.' He raised an eyebrow. 'There'd be a lot of relief in Downing Street if we did, sir. No concessions to the French . . .'

The director smiled. 'That'll be the day, Jones! Now, where will you start?'

'The only place we know of, Champbiére where it all happened.'

'And who are you going to use?'

Rigbey sat forward in his chair.

'Me, I hope, sir.'

The director looked at him speculatively and with slight distaste. No one could blame Rigbey but he was really the cause of all this. Without him there would have been no pressure.

'You are out in front, certainly, Rigbey – out in the open, as it were. But you'll need a team behind you.' He turned to Jones.

'Who have we got available?'

'Usual man-and-woman team, sir?'

The director nodded.

'Well, sir, there's the Hardinge girl.'

'Hardinge or Hardwicke?'

'I *was* thinking of Hardinge, sir.'

The director thought for a moment, making flicking noises with his tongue against his front teeth, then shook his head. 'No, Sarah's as good as we've got but it's too soon after Prague. Let the scars heal a bit. What about the Hardwicke girl, though?'

'It will be her first big operation.'

'Have you anyone better?'

'No, sir.'

'Then we'll give Tassie a chance. Now what about men?'

'Tim Jolling?'

'We need him for the Turkish operation.'

'Ferrando?'

'Too much invested in his background. We can't blow an unknown unless we need complete anonymity. This is going to be a strike, not an infiltration.'

'Then it will have to be Mark Evelyn. He's the best heavy we've got.'

The director made shuffling movements with the papers on the table in front of him. 'Well, that's that then. Set it up, Jones. James here out in front and Evelyn and Hardwicke behind.' He smiled at Rigbey.

'A week is longer than we usually get, James.' Then, to Jones 'You'd better get on to Tassie and Mark.'

.   .   .   .   .

Eight hours later and five hundred miles away, the Inspector of Police at Champbiére glanced at Glasiére and pursed his lips.

'Do you mean, monsieur, that I am to do less than my best to obtain the release of this woman?'

Glasiére was exasperated. He had no time for men who were unable to compromise.

'You put it crudely, Inspector, but that is generally what I was trying to convey. There are excellent reasons why your superiors would not wish the woman to be found or released within the next seven days. After that you may use every effort.'

The inspector's face showed its contempt.

'Monsieur, when I first became a *gendarme* I swore an oath. You are asking me to break that oath.'

'I am asking you only to co-operate.'

'I regret, monsieur, that I cannot do so without an order.'

Glasiére drew in his breath.

'You have that order.'

'In writing, monsieur.'

Glasiére's hand was shaking as he drew a ball-point pen from his inner pocket and wrote on the pad that the inspector pushed across the desk.

The inspector looked at the writing critically.

'Inspector Beyer is requested to act with less than customary vigour in conducting the search for Mme Juliette Montague presently believed to have been kidnapped.'

The inspector crossed out the word 'requested' and substituted 'instructed'. He pushed the pad back across the table. Glasiére's face was red with fury but he signed against the alteration. The Brits would be here any time now and this policeman with a conscience was being difficult!

4

The girl in the hut in the French Alps had folded toilet paper into narrow strips and wound it round the anklets but it was the weight that hurt. The chains hung down, solid, resting on the swell of her heel and on the ankle bone, rubbing and chafing at the skin. It was Saturday night and almost two days since she had bathed. She could smell the stale sweat that came up from the neck of her jumper. The men kept the stove at its maximum heat, day and night. She laid down a king and took the trick, looking apologetically at Videl as she did so. They were playing solo whist and she was winning.

Videl watched her as they played. It would soon be time to hurt her again. She had behaved perfectly all day, shuffling round the shack, tidying things away and cooking their two meals. This was the danger. The lecturers had been specific. After a time the captors became too friendly with their hostages – couldn't pile on the hate when the time came, couldn't hurt their newly found friends. You had to keep up the hate – make them fear you and despise them for their fear. You *had* to do that. Then you could kill or mutilate if you had to. Videl led a card.

Juliette felt her stomach contracting and swallowed to force down the rising fear. She knew the signs. Something cruel was on its way; she had seen the same expression on her husband's face, the same tension in his shoulders and fingers as he worked himself up into the state that ended in violence.

Videl looked up at the end of the round.

'Coffee, Juliette? I think we would all like some.'

38

She got up from the table and walked to the stove with the short steps her chain allowed. The coffee-pot had been drawn to one side but it was three-quarters full. She turned four cups upright and poured the coffee, put the cups on a faded tin tray and carried them back to the table. Beppo's eyes were on her legs, watching, fascinated as the chain dragged on the floor at each step. She put the tray down and raised her eyes to find Videl staring at her. She felt a quick prickle of perspiration.

It was going to be now. Make it quick! *Please* make it quick! It was going to hurt but let it be quick.

Videl stood up slowly and moved round the table. She stood, arms by her side, waiting for him. He reached out and took a handful of her hair from behind her head pulling at it until her head was forced back, chin up in the air. He went on pulling and she reached out to hold the table as she sank down awkwardly on to her knees. His voice was gentle.

'Juliette – you must never serve yourself unless you are told to.'

Swiftly he struck – right hand, left hand across her cheeks. Her head jerked sideways then .back again.

'Now go away, Juliette.' She started to get up.

'No, Juliette, as you are. You crawl there.'

She turned and began to crawl on her hands and knees. Her skirt was too long and she had to pause every few seconds to pull it out from under her legs. Splinters from the rough boards tore at her skin and the dirt caked soles of her feet showed black as she dragged herself towards the bedroom.

Vosper sat back in his chair and smiled slowly. Beppo leaned forward staring at her rump as it moved under her clothes. Videl waited until she reached up to turn the door handle before he gathered up the cards and shuffled them. The three of them began to play.

In the bedroom the girl pulled herself up on to the bed and lay with her cheek pillowed on her arms, sobbing her relief.

It hadn't been too bad at all. She thought back over the hell of her five years of marriage. Videl didn't even begin to compare with her husband. She wondered if he was really a pervert or if he was just going through a routine to keep her cowed. It was almost as if he was doing it from a textbook. There would be more cruelty later on; it was inevitable. Then she would be able to tell. She rolled over on to her back, the chain making soft clinking noises, and clasped her hands behind her head. There were six more days. She smiled grimly. Unless Videl stepped up the cruelties and humiliations, she was nowhere near the boundaries of her tolerance. Then she laughed out loud at a thought. So she had *something* to be thankful to her husband for. He had given her an excellent training.

Her brain had unfrozen and she was thinking hard; plotting, planning, testing devious stratagems in her mind, trying out potential lies to see if they were safe – just as she had when she was married. With three of them there she could do nothing except placate them, keep the hurting to a minimum. But a week was a long time and she might be left with two of them, which might be possible, or even one. And then . . . !

She waited an hour, then took up the long-handled brush and went out into the living room. Vosper and Beppo looked at her idly as she began to sweep. She continued brushing towards the back door. She was looking for something which she knew must be in the hut, but which they had concealed so successfully that two days of sweeping and tidying had failed to find it.

Videl had been in the privy and, as she opened the back door, he was washing himself in the icy water that came from the heavily lagged pipe in the lean-to. He had a plastic wet-pack toilet case on the table by the tap. It had a solid base with a zip running round it. She turned her head so that he shouldn't see the gleam of satisfaction in her eyes. The brush strokes became firmer and quicker and she sang under her breath. Videl looked at her in surprise.

Beppo had watched the girl as she swept the floor of the hut. The swinging movement of her arms brought her jumper taut against her breasts and Beppo felt the saliva oozing into his mouth as he watched them quiver. He wondered if Videl would hurt her again. He had felt a surge of excitement that had almost made him cry out when Videl had struck her. He reached for his magazine and turned to the picture of a naked girl, bound and gagged. He imagined her in that state and tossed the magazine away convulsively. He had to move, do something to ease the tension that was building up inside him. He got up and walked to the window, feeling the draught that blew through the badly fitting frame cold on his belly. The tension eased. But it still wasn't fair – keeping him shut up with that woman and not allowed to touch. He remembered the feel of her thighs as he had lain across them when Videl was chaining her. He stuck his hands fiercely in his pockets and gripped himself through the cloth.

The girl had seen him move and had gone to the near corner of the shack so that she could watch him while she swept. She saw the rhythmically moving hands under the clothes. The man was nearly going spare. She smiled grimly. 'Beppo, my friend, take care.' She almost said the words aloud, then let the animation die out of her eyes. Six more days! She began to plan the details.

5

It was Sunday afternoon and Johann Walther came down from his bedroom above the butcher's shop dressed in a track-suit. He was adjusting the sweat-band over his forehead. His hair was a lot longer than he cared for, but those were the instructions. 'Look ordinary and sloppy.' He was late.

He let himself out of the side door by the shop and started jogging immediately. It was cold and he needed the warmth from the exercise. He took two left turns and then ran hard to catch the bus that was pulling away from its stop. The driver slowed and opened the hydraulic doors to let him in.

It was half an hour to the gathering spot and he could see the others within a minute of leaving the bus. He was one of the last and, five minutes later, they were off, a pack of twenty, mostly young men with a scattering of thirty-year-olds and a couple of girls out for an invigorating Sunday-afternoon marathon in the mountains that lie to the south of Munich. An ordinary and praiseworthy expedition.

On Mondays a pistol-club met in a cellar in the old part of the town. It was an enthusiastic body of young people – though, again, a few were past their twenties. The range of weapons was surprising and evidenced the wealth of their members, or their backers.

On Tuesdays an evening class in chemistry was held in the laboratory of a small private pharmaceutical firm. The curriculum was highly specialized and would have created a great deal of interest in police circles, if the students had not been so discreet.

On Wednesdays a study group met and heard lectures on the political and administrative structures of the principal states of Europe. There was no indoctrination – far from it, the lecturers were exceedingly objective and cynical about their subject.

On Thursdays more specialized lectures were given. By a stretch of etymology they could be called lectures in psychology, but of a very particular kind.

Fridays and Saturdays were for ordinary pursuits.

The membership of all these groups was identical, although it was drawn from people who lived in various parts of the city and its suburbs. They were dedicated young people and they had a purpose. They were the Munich pack of the Wolves.

.　　.　　.　　.　　.　　.

Sunday was also a good day for the higher council. The top board members had their own individual position to keep up during the week and a week-end gave them the anonymity and facility for secret journeys. The conference room in the tall office block in Geneva was soundproof and totally bug-free.

Apart from Fafner, there were four members of the higher council and they had taken the names of great composers from their own countries. Gluck was a manufacturer of heavy machinery in the Ruhr. Elgar was the head of one of the big pharmaceutical firms in Britain and Donnizetti ran a motor empire in Italy.

43

Ravel was a banker of Paris. Fafner looked round the table and searched the faces of his companions. It was impossible that one of them could be the betrayer. These were the shareholders, the men who made the enormous profits of the enterprise, the men who stood to lose enormous sums if disaster occurred. Their faces were bland. They were men who could always be secure in their own conceit. Theirs were always the policy decisions. Anything that went wrong could always be blamed on the executives. Their knowledge of detail was small; their instincts and judgement were of the highest quality. They were discussing recruitment. Fafner spoke.

'My friends, our groups in Glasgow and North London are now operational. Thirty men and four women in the former and fifteen men and two women in the latter. The Central London Group has now effectively split with close on twenty people in each. The Birmingham and Swansea groups are on the move and we should have two more in London by the year end. This brings the total number of our personnel throughout Europe to two thousand and seventy-four divided into eighty-seven groups.'

Elgar spoke. Both he and the French banker had held high rank in the services. His voice was pedantic and carried the harsh bray of the Thames Valley.

'That is all very well, Fafner, but I feel we must not use these forces piecemeal. The fiasco with the school bus will have lowered morale throughout the organization. We must expect our disasters but in a concerted effort by all the packs at once the odd disgrace will be wiped out by the successes.'

Fafner nodded. He picked up another cigar and rolled it in his fingers before lighting it.

'I think we all agree with you when it comes to direct action but our greatest successes are from the indirect actions of our groups. The industrial unrest in Britain and Italy has become progressively more violent and we can expect it to reach a state of near-anarchy within the next year. Perhaps we should remind ourselves of our main objects.'

He paused and ran his tongue over his lips. They were full lips, with a brightness that went with the fleshy face. When he spoke again his voice was soft and the two at the end of the table leaned forward to listen.

'Europe, my friends, is soft. The protection that the very awfulness of atomic warfare has given to the people of this Continent has sapped their will-power. They no longer feel strongly about anything except their own materialistic society which they will go to any lengths to protect. They have now become accustomed to the idea that force pays and there is no one who will withstand properly directed force. Let there be any weakening on the part of an aggressor and they will turn upon him and rend him. But let him show a bold face and demonstrate in the clearest terms that he will back up his threats with action, then they will find reasons to comply with him and placate him. We have all seen the success of the terrorist groups; how governments will treat with them and give way, lose their dignity and grovel rather than be seen to endanger their people.'

He paused for effect.

'We intend to make the major countries of Europe so accustomed to violence and terror that we will be able to take over from within. Take over, not the governments; we do not want to govern, but the means

45

to wealth. We will make our own rules, we will operate as we wish and we will crush opposition. The people will placate us. They will fear us and they will obey us. All this we will do within the next two years. But recruitment must come first. We need ten thousand. Give me that and we can move.'

Gluck cut in. He had three chins and they gobbled as he spoke.

'And that is why we must have a success — something that will bring them flocking in — we must *never* have another such disaster.' He turned to Fafner.

'Do we yet know how the failure with the bus occurred?'

Fafner sat with his hands clasped on the table. He waited for a long moment until the others began to shuffle in their seats.

'By the end of the week we should know.'

'And then?'

'And then the danger will be eliminated.'

.   .   .   .   .

The palms of Claude Manet's hands had begun to sweat. He was on the safe phone and Glasiére's voice was compelling. He tried again.

'But, monsieur, surely I am your most valuable source of information. How can you do without me? I am your only lead into the Wolves organization.'

'Claude, my friend — think of yourself as a famous footballer. We are putting you on the transfer list. We shall do very well out of the bargain, believe me. But we have your safety to think of. We have their promise that you will be unharmed . . .' He laughed, '. . . but we would wish to be sure, would we not?'

Claude put the phone down slowly. He had five days in which to make his preparations. On the sixth day he must go. Except they would be expecting him to go on the sixth day. He felt a wave of revulsion sweep over him. After all he'd done! And now they were going to throw him to the Wolves.

Claude consulted his very special notebook before he picked up the phone again. He had to dial twice before he got the number he wanted. Graugin's voice was thick with booze.

'Claude? Claude?' Then recollection. 'Why, Claude, my old one. After all these years. How goes it, friend?'

Graugin had been in the Legion with Manet. They had fought together in Algeria and Manet had come back to take the government side in the near-revolution that had followed the war. Graugin had gone the other way; the way of the individualist. He had kept his contacts on the southern edge of the Mediterranean and he ran a boat from Bandol, a small seaside town near Marseilles.

Claude Manet began to speak rapidly, masking his fear with the old argot of the Legionnaire. He paused and listened to the reassuring words that came back over the wire and he felt relief flood over him. Trust Graugin! The one truly reliable man he knew. Graugin would get him out.

· · · · ·

In the Gendarmerie at Champbiére, James Rigbey was doing his best to save Claude Manet's life but he was getting precious little help from the French police. Inspector Beyer's face was cold.

'It is simply not possible, monsieur. To search the mountains would require a whole Alpine Division and surely you must realize that the woman is far away by now.'

Rigbey was patient.

'It is possible, of course, but it is unlikely she has crossed a frontier. She is almost certainly still in France.'

'True, monsieur, though not certain. But why here? Why not far away.'

'Because I was there within an hour of old Pierre's death. I was early – Videl said so. She hadn't been long gone and I had come up the road from Champbiére.'

'True, but the main road goes on to Geneva; they could have turned the other way.'

Rigbey shook his head.

'But the snow, Beyer. The snow! I would have seen the tracks coming down the road from Pierre's place and no vehicle had been on that road since the snow started. But there *had* been a four-wheel drive outside the house and Videl came back *down* the valley in just such a vehicle.'

Beyer shrugged. 'Perhaps so but they could have transhipped her on the way. We don't know. . . .'

Rigbey looked the policeman in the eyes.

'No, we don't know, monsieur, but we could find out. Tell me, monsieur, have you had any special instructions on how much or little you should co-operate with us?'

Beyer's face flushed and he held Rigbey's eyes for only a moment before he got up and moved round his desk, holding out his hand.

'Good-day, M. Rigbey.' Then . . . 'You may be assured that when the time is right you will have my full co-operation.'

Rigbey left the Gendarmerie and walked back to the

Coq d'Or where the strike group had established itself. He collected his key at the desk and climbed to his room on the first floor. Evelyn and the Hardwicke girl were already there. Mark standing by the window, a heavy man, violet eyes restless and searching while the girl was curled up on his bed reading a magazine. Her blonde hair was caught in a pony tail. She was tall with a sturdy figure and she looked at Rigbey calmly, blue eyes asking the question.

Rigbey shook his head.

'Well, that's the second time I've seen them and they aren't going to help. They want our bargain to stick and they are obviously prepared to lose their man in the process. Poor bloody pawn!'

'So what now?'

Rigbey sat in the armchair, stretched out his legs and clasped his hands behind his head.

'So we do the job ourselves.' He twisted his wrist and looked at his watch. 'Crack of dawn tomorrow. Beyer said you'd need an Alpine Division to search those mountains.' He smiled. 'Well . . . even allowing for a little exaggeration that means plenty.'

6

Streicher pulled up outside the hut. The engine of the Mercedes made hardly any sound but he had been heard. He could see the hurried movements behind the window curtains. He smiled to himself as he walked towards the door. The orders he carried were sensible. They got jittery if they didn't get a break.

The door opened a crack then Videl came out of the hut to join him.

'All well?'

'Yes, all well!'

'Very good. You may come down into the town for the evening and you can allow each of the others to have a break – one evening each.'

Videl's eyes were cold.

'I don't need any breaks. Neither do the others. We will stay here and not expose ourselves.'

Streicher stared at him. The man looked afraid.

'You will surely do as you are ordered?'

Videl's eyes flickered and then dropped.

'Why is it necessary? Rigbey could be there. He knows me.'

Streicher smiled. 'Rigbey will not be there. We have the area covered and we will know if anyone turns up. Now, Videl, you will leave the hut for rest and recreation, Vosper will go tomorrow evening and Beppo the day after that. Understood?'

Videl nodded slowly. 'I will follow you down.'

He turned and went back into the hut. The girl had been thrust into the bedroom and Vosper was with her. He called him out into the living room and began to whisper, as they heard Streicher's car start up.

Streicher was only mildly uneasy as he drove back to Champbiére. Four days before the operation had begun, a dozen young men and women from the Geneva pack had obtained temporary jobs in the town to be ready as a back-up group during the operation. The council member for the Geneva pack had been left in ignorance of their purpose. Council members could not be trusted; not until the end of the week. This was a job for the top, for people like himself and Videl who were headquarters men. He turned the car into the parking area of the chalet that had been rented on the outskirts of Champbiére.

There was excitement in the eyes of the young woman who sat in the chalet's living room. She was still wearing her thick grey mantle with its hood thrown back. She had been warming her hands by the stove and she rubbed them together as she rose to greet him. Streicher felt a thrill of apprehension.

'Yes?'

'They are here. At least we think they are.'

It was her first experience of active service and she had no assurance.

'Who is here? What do you mean?' Streicher's voice was sharp. 'Make your report properly, as you have been taught.'

The girl swallowed and paused, collecting her thoughts.

'A man who looks like Rigbey. He is going openly to the Gendarmerie. He has been twice today. But there are two others. A man and a girl. They are English. They look like lovers and the girl is taking the pill but the man is a . . .' She faltered, searching for the precision she knew would be required. '. . . Well – it is said he has a "hard" look and there is a locked bag that cannot be opened with our keys. They have not been seen speaking to Rigbey but they have a room directly below his.'

The girl stopped and looked at Streicher for approval. She was in her early twenties and had the freckled face and pallid skin that went with her auburn hair.

Streicher had not moved. He was standing with shoulders hunched, hands thrust deep in his pockets, staring at the stove. He was thinking hard. He had

51

slipped badly. He should have checked reports before he went up to the hut.

'Where is he now?'

'At the Coq d'Or.'

'When did you leave?'

'Twenty minutes ago but there are two others there, outside. They would have come, or phoned if he had moved.'

Streicher nodded.

'Good. Stay here and take messages.' He turned and left the room, half running as he crunched across the snow-covered gravel to his car. He drove hard back towards the mountain hut and Videl.

．　　．　　．　　．　　．

Videl was seething with fear as he drove towards Champbiére. He preferred to call it rage but it was truly fear. He felt no need for recreation, he wished only to hide, to stay away from the danger that must now be roaming all Western Europe, the hard men of the security services who would kill and who would not scruple in obtaining information from him if he was found. He saw the headlights bouncing towards him up the secondary road, sending flashes of light into the air. He pulled the vehicle well over to the right. It could hardly be them, coming so openly and so swiftly and in one car. He felt a moment of pure terror as the approaching vehicle stopped, then he saw Streicher's head stuck out of the driver's window.

'Videl! You were right, my friend. Rigbey is in Champbiére and there are a couple of others with him.'

Videl felt his bowels yearning. His voice was shrill.

'What did I tell you? They know something!'

'Quiet, my friend. Be tranquil. They suspect but they do not know. There is no sign of activity from the French and we must give them a diversion.'

Videl was suspicious.

'A diversion?'

'Yes, my friend. You will divert them for us. You and I are the only ones they know and I have chosen you to lead them away.'

'You mean *I* am going to be out in front. Out in the open?'

'Yes, you, Videl. But we will not let them harm you. You will not move until tomorrow and by then we will have arranged protection for you.' He smiled. 'Now, Videl, can you trust the two of them to hold the girl for a couple of days?'

Videl was only half thinking of the girl, the rest of his mind was concentrating on his own predicament.

'Yes, I think so. She will probably be raped by Beppo. Would that matter?'

'No. It would not matter. Indeed it would help. She is to be thoroughly cowed before you leave. Be sure she has no spirit left, no will to escape. Understood?'

'Yes, understood.'

'I will come for you tomorrow evening. Be brave, my friend, you will be well cared for.'

'Why not tonight?'

'Because we must have time to arrange things.'

Streicher withdrew his head and reversed, his snow chains clattering on the stones. Videl watched him turn and go before swinging the heavy vehicle round and pointing it back up to the shack.

He saw the anxious face peering through the crack in the curtains and he waved a reassuring hand as he climbed out of the driver's seat. He stamped his feet

53

as he walked through the two inches of snow. Only Beppo was in the living room when he opened the door. Vosper would be with the girl. He nodded towards the bedroom.

'Call him. Leave the girl.'

He took them out through the back door in the shelter of the lean-to where they would not be overheard.

'There are security men in Champbiére.'

He watched for their reaction. Vosper's stare hardened and there was a flicker of fear in Beppo's eyes.

Videl had already become accustomed to the idea of playing the hero. 'I will be leading them away, tomorrow. Do you think you can hold the girl for two days?'

He saw the interest on Beppo's face. Vosper would be no hindrance, he would either watch cynically or keep out of the way. When Beppo had finished with her she would have no spirit left, her soul would have gone. But it was Vosper who answered him.

'Yes, we can hold her. Do we have to be gentle?'

Videl smiled. 'There will be no need to be otherwise. I shall hurt her badly tonight and she will be no trouble until I get back.' His smile broadened. He laughed out loud and motioned the other two back into the hut. He pushed past them, towards the bedroom and the girl. It was late but he had work to do. The bedroom door swung to behind him and Beppo felt his blood quicken as the girl began to scream.

7

Monday was a day for reading papers. In London
Captain Jones sat in his office off St James's Street and
picked up his first file. He was trying to read the build-
up for the operation in Turkey but his mind kept
straying back to the French Alps. Finally, he gave in
and pursed his lips. He pressed the red buzzer. Sarah
Hardinge was doing a week as security officer and she
came into his room looking worn. Jones smiled at her.

'Good week-end, Sarah?'

She had dark mousy hair and a mole on her chin. It
was the life in her eyes that made her face – that and
the well-fed gamin look, made more interesting by the
hair-line scar that ran from the outer corner of her eye
to the edge of her mouth. She had good legs. She
yawned.

'Fine, thanks, Captain Jones. These lawyers don't half
expect their pound of flesh, though.' Sarah had recently
taken up with a practising barrister and had calmly
accepted the security check that had been done on him.
She had read it afterwards with great glee, except for
the bit where his wife had died.

Jones smiled.

'Sarah, could you get me everything on the French
Alps, please?'

'You mean the Wolves job?'

'Please.'

Five minutes later he was going through everything
again. He had seen it all on the morning and evening
summaries but he wanted to see the lot all together.

It was a thick file and there would soon be a second
volume. The reports were coming in fast from all the

friendly countries. Wolf packs were known to exist at eighteen different points in Europe, which meant that sixty-nine had so far escaped detection. For two hours he read through the files, picking up the feel of the Wolves. There were no reports of any packs in Great Britain and, finally, he sat back in his chair and stared at the ceiling for a moment before leaning forward and picking up the phone.

Mealie Jimmy had only just got in at the Yard. He had spent most of the week-end quarrelling with his wife and he was abrasive, the flat northern vowels adding a smack of malice to his words.

'No, Jones. I've told you before and I've checked again, there's no question of a Wolf pack in Britain. There was one small operation which might have been them, but it was put down to the Frogs or the Krauts.'

He listened impatiently then . . . 'Damn it, Jones, can't you take "No"? I tell you there are no packs in Britain. If there were, we'd have heard about them by now.'

He stared at the framed picture of himself outside the Palace holding his CBE in its velvet-lined box, grinning at the photographer. He began to pull at the hairs that sprouted from the pink birthmark on his chin. He grunted into the phone every five seconds as Jones spoke, then interrupted him. He hated professional soldiers and particularly those who wore civilian clothes. He took it as his duty to bring them down off their high horses.

'Now get this straight, Jones. We all know you security people look over your shoulders all the time in case there's a little green man sitting there but I'll tell you, the only bloody wolf packs in Britain wear khaki shorts and caps and give two-fingered salutes. Do you get the message, Jones? Two-fingered salutes!'

Jones put the phone down gently. He felt Mealie Jimmy in his stomach, squirting acid as though he was the active constituent of an ulcer. He shook his head and smiled as he thought of some of the shits he had known in his time.

There was a knock and Sarah Hardinge came in. He wondered once more just what it was that made her so attractive to men. He took a quick glance at her legs. It couldn't be just that? Her smile was certainly a come-on. He caught his thoughts back.

'Maureen in registry thinks you ought to look at this one, Captain Jones.'

She held out a green loose-folder that protected and identified material that had not yet been classified. Jones took it and read the note inside. He looked up at Sarah and smiled ruefully.

'What made Maureen send this in?'

'Oh!, you know Maureen, reads everthing she files. She said this had the right feel about it. Same MO as the European packs – labs and lectures and so on.' Sarah's imitation of Maureen's throaty wheeze broadened Jones's smile.

The North London Wolf Pack had slipped up badly. They had been in the middle of a chemistry lecture in a laboratory in Camden Town when the caretaker had come into the lab. He had left his keys behind and the lecturer had paused politely while the caretaker had limped painfully round the room to retrieve the key-ring.

Had the Wolf pack watched the caretaker on Remembrance Day they would have seen him wearing the ribbon of the George Medal. Had they checked far beyond the boundaries of prudence, far beyond the most absurd limits of caution, they would have found that he had won the medal and acquired the limp and stiff left arm in a bomb-disposal unit during the war. They all saw his start and the quick appraising glance he gave to the equipment on the table but they put it down to his embarrassment at interrupting them. This sort of thing had happened to most Wolf packs and standing instructions said you carried on normally and gave no indications of alarm.

Now Jones was reading the police report. They were treating it lightly. There were so many bomb scares and the circumstances didn't fit. A very respectable organization, the police said. They hadn't checked the people out yet but, from the description of the care-taker, they were a responsible lot, no sign of outside influences. However, they would be obliged if security would check it out for them.

Jones looked at Sarah, who nodded encouragingly. Damn the woman — she'd be mothering him next. His voice was terse as he handed the file back to her.

'Probably nothing but get it over to Mealie Jimmy. Might as well stir him up a bit.'

Sarah went out grinning.

. . . . .

The new building of New Scotland Yard gives a good view over south-western London. Consultants have some of the best rooms and Mealie Jimmy was standing by the plate-glass window looking over the grime of Victoria. He was pulling again at the hairs on his birth-mark — each morning he shaved round it carefully. His back was aching, low down on the right hand side. He put a hand under his jacket and rubbed.

There was a tap at the door. Mealie Jimmy moved to his desk and sat down. One of the clever lads came in. Degree in Sociology for Sweet Robert's sake. Probably tried to charm the little bastards when he did his two years on the beat. Looking down his nose now, as though there was a bad smell in the room. College education! There was too much of that these days. Better put him in his place.

'Something wrong, Deckham?'

'No, sir.'

Mealie Jimmy stared at him for a moment, then lay back in his chair. This new furniture was a bit better than the old wooden armchairs with padded arms he'd had in the north. Deckham was still standing, hands clasped in front of him, looking like a ballet dancer.

'Deckham, you're going to sweat your miserable little guts out today, my boy.' He paused, waiting for the lad to squirm. There was no expression on his face.

'Ever heard of the Wolves, lad?'

'Yes, sir.'

Damn him, who'd he think he was with his two years on the beat, two more in traffic and a special detachment in Jubilee year when he'd made his one and only big pinch. Accelerated promotion! He thought of his own ten years as a constable before the great day had come and he'd begun to rise. Everything easy these days. Get everything on a plate. He let his eyelids drop over the pig's fat.

'*What* do you know, Deckham?'

'Highly organized terrorist organization thought to be operating exclusively on the Continent up to now. Aims unknown and no declared objects but always operating under terrorist conditions. Every operation treated as being on full war footing. Central control unknown but the French infiltrated their lower operational committee and tipped off the Germans about the school-bus hijack. Some people think it was a pity they didn't let it go on, then we'd have known what they were after, but there *were* forty kids involved.' Deckham looked at the consultant with mild contempt. 'They get funds from straightforward robbery – always successful, except once and then the two survivors took cyanide before they could be questioned.'

Jimmy watched his subordinate, eyes still narrowed. Too clever by half, this boy.

'You said "*thought* to be operating on the Continent up to now". Don't *you* think so?'

Deckham's lips stretched into a thin line.

'I have no opinion, sir. The evidence shows there have been no . . .'

'Damn the evidence, Deckham, save that for the twisting lawyers when you're in the box. Tell me, man. What do you *think*, and *why*! We've *said* they don't operate here and I'll fry anyone who's let me down.'

Deckham was getting tired of standing. He put his hands behind his back and made the almost imperceptible muscle relaxing genuflection, the slight easing of the knees, that all beat constables learn in their first six months.

He collected his thoughts. There must be no sloppiness now.

'There *is* no evidence, sir, but we *have* had whispers. Only whispers. There's something going on up over the border and there's something here in London.' He saw the impatience leap into the consultant's eyes and went on hurriedly before he could be interrupted.

'Sir! I said there was no evidence. Nothing to go on at all but there are good men on our side who think something big is building up. They daren't put it in their reports because they'd be asked what there was to go on and there's nothing. Nothing, that is . . .' He broke off and looked nervously up at the corner of the room.

'Nothing, that is, but what?' Mealie Jimmy could feel he was getting there. The same feeling he had had thousands of times during forty years as a copper. He had been right considerably more than half the time.

'Sir, you probably don't know Brass Turnbull. He's a Soho heavy and never comes our side of the pool. He's called "Brass" because he's fond of the knuckles. He's hard, sir, really hard, but he did his time in the Commandos during the war and turns out with a Union Jack when the Queen goes by – smashed in the face of a Maltese who said she looked like a horse. Anyway, sir, he put in a whisper. Asked one of the lads on his manor to get a Special Branch man to him. He said something about Wolf cubs and he laughed when he said it.' Deckham's eyes began to blink rapidly.

'When the Special Branch man reached him, Turnbull was crying – weeping, sir. He saw him in his room in Wardour Street. Turnbull just sat there crying and wouldn't say a word.'

'It's not in pattern, lad. You know that.'

Jimmy's eyes were mere slits.

'I know, sir. If it's the Wolves and they're as good as they say, they'd have killed him.'

'Then why didn't they?'

'I don't know, sir.' Deckham waited for the foul-mouthed scorn but the consultant's voice was soft.

'Right, lad, nothing to go on, as you say, but we're not ordinary coppers on this floor, are we? Now you take a sergeant and start sniffing around. Then lay on an operation to check this out.' He tossed the report Jones had sent him on to the desk. 'Start with Turnbull and his associates and move on from there but get this laboratory checked.' His eyes snapped. 'And try and look less like a bloody Sunday School teacher, man.'

Deckham felt his eyes prickling as he left the room. His loathing for the consultant was matched only by his contempt for his blatant self-seeking. He saw the eyes avoiding him as he got back to the room he shared with the others.

.   .   .   .   .

In Geneva Wolfgang Fafner was sleeping late and he lay with his mouth open. His secretary moved in the great bed to avoid his breath. She turned her head and looked at the digital clock on the bedside table. Ten-thirty but, then, it had been past two a.m. when they had finished in the planning room. Gently she wriggled to the side of the bed and lifted the bedclothes so that she could swing her legs out. The heavy warmth of the air-conditioning allowed her to wear a cambric night-dress. It had elaborate vari-coloured smocking at the breast and the hem came down to her ankles. The care-fully pedicured feet that showed beneath the cloth were pink and strangely petite in such a woman.

She crossed to the window and pulled on the heavy cord that dragged back the curtains. It was a pale day but the weak sunlight was enough to wake Fafner. He rolled over in bed and felt the warm emptiness where the woman had lain. He opened his eyes and saw her silhouetted by a shaft of sunlight which penetrated the thin material of her nightgown. It was a sturdy figure but satisfying. There were no unseemly bulges and he caught the upturned line of a firm breast. Not bad for forty-four. She turned and smiled at him and Fafner felt one of his rare moments of sentiment.

Inge Ludwig crossed to the door and lifted down the heavy quilted dressing gown. She had slept far too late and she was annoyed with herself as she put her feet into fur mules and stepped out into the corridor. She walked to the door at the end and went into the nursery. The Swedish nurse looked up and smiled. She was feeding the boy with a spoon while the girl was struggling with a knife and fork. She was six and the boy almost four. The two children greeted her rapturously and she bent and put an arm round each of them, pressing her cheek to their foreheads in turn. They were trilingual but they spoke in French and they called her Maman.

8

In France the strike group was preparing for its search of the mountains. Mark Evelyn felt a slight guilt. They had been in Champbiére more than twenty hours and nothing to show for it.

James Rigbey snapped the slightly oiled magazine into his Browning and slid the weapon into his shoulder holster. The holster was open at the bottom to take the silencer. The courier from the embassy had been waiting for them when they arrived and they were now equipped with their own combat arms. Two cars had also been provided.

They left in Rigbey's car as the sun was coming up. They were a strike group and secrecy was not essential. Four kilometres from Champbiére, Rigbey swung left on to the secondary road that led past Pierre Pecheur's house. A niece had arrived and taken possession and there was smoke coming from the chimney once more.

It was a loop road connecting two main roads that ran to the border and thence to Geneva. It was ten kilometres long and it gave access to farms like Pecheur's that were scattered up the valley and, after eight kilometres, to a tiny hamlet, no more than a dozen houses, that boasted one ski lift. The snow-plough had been out and the road was almost clear.

They had planned the operation over an early break-fast. They would drive to the far end of the valley and work back down it to Pecheur's house. It would take them two days to cover the ground and from Wednes-day they would cross the main road at the far end and start on the three valleys that spread out like fingers into the next range of mountains.

Rigbey knew the Alps.

'There are huts up in higher valleys. They take the cattle up there in summer and camp out. If she's in this valley, it will almost certainly be in one of those. The map shows at least a dozen.'

He pulled up in sight of the far trunk road and backed carefully, turning the car to face towards Champbiére. Tassie had the map spread on her lap.

'Half a kilometre more and there's the first track. No hut marked but that doesn't mean there won't be one, does it?'

Rigbey shook his head.

'No – we start here.' He pulled off the road and put on the handbrake.

The snow was no more than a couple of inches thick

64

and their climbing boots with the pyramid nails bit through the thin crust. Rigbey went out in front, two hundred yards ahead of the others. They had come with the standard mountain and snow operation kits and all three were wearing white snow smocks and snow goggles and compared with a man in ordinary clothes they were virtually invisible. They each took one side of the valley and followed Rigbey – a probing triangle ready to kill.

The valley wound to the right and then branched into two. At the head of the right fork was a hut. Rigbey saw it first and motioned to the others to approach with caution.

They were in good cover and they stared at the wooden shack. There was no smoke from the chimney. Rigbey held up a hand then went forward, making no effort at concealment. He walked up to the side of the hut, peered in through a window then went on round the back. They saw him waving to them and they closed up.

'Nothing here. No footprints. Place abandoned for the winter. Back to the car.'

It took twenty minutes to get back to their vehicle and another five to drive to the beginning of the next track. This time it was a substantial farmhouse, set well back up on the slope of the mountain. Rigbey waited until the other two had made their way up the hill on foot before driving up the farm track.

The mistress of the house was no more than thirty. She was wearing a black and grey checked slack suit and she beamed her pleasure.

Yes, they had accommodation for skiers but the nearest ski lift was two kilometres away. She promised a warm welcome, however, and all for sixty francs a night. Her eyes said that a lot more might be had for free. She would look forward to Rigbey's letter. She smiled and waved as he left, then sighed and went back to the baby crying in the cot.

For the next fifteen minutes Mark and Tassie kept watch on the house waiting for movements once the immediate danger had passed. There was nothing. It took them half an hour to work their way back to Rigbey's car. He was waiting for them with a flask of coffee. He looked at their flushed faces.

'Beyer was right. We're going to need a division to search the mountains properly.' They rested another ten minutes then set out for the next valley.

Far up the mountainside a young German, also clad in a white snow cape, slid his binoculars back into their case and turned to his skis, propped against the rocky outcrop. When his breathless phone call reached Geneva, Fafner thought for a moment, then said, 'Get the diversion into operation fast.'

The snow was falling again in the mountains as the light began to fail and the strike group drove back to Champbiére. It settled in fat flakes on the bonnet of the car, melted, and shuddered sideways in ridged pools of water. They were all tired and Rigbey was beginning to have doubts. They had covered a third of the possible hiding places by dusk and they would rapidly get within an impossibly short distance of Pierre Pecheur's house the next morning. They reached the main road, turned right for the run into Champbiére and the going became easier until they got behind a truck and Rigbey dropped back to avoid the sludge that was thrown up by its wheels.

Two pairs of eyes watched them as they drove into the far outskirts of the town. A minute later the girl in

Streicher's chalet picked up the phone, listened intently for a moment, then replaced the receiver. She took a list of ten numbers from her handbag and began dialling.

A bearded young man of twenty lifted the phone in his lodging house, listened, acknowledged the message, went to the shed in the back garden and started up the engine of his scooter. He drove carefully down through the main square of Champbiére and on to its southern outskirt. He stopped at a café and hauled the bike on to its stand. He went into the café, kicking the snow from his shoes. Videl felt his scalp prickle as he saw the boy. He folded his newspaper and laid it carefully on his corner table. The boy made no attempt to speak to Videl but stood at the bar and ordered a coffee. As it was set in front of him Videl got up and went out to his car. The diversion had started.

He drove slowly up to the main square and pulled up outside the café that faced the Coq d'Or. The man in the van parked to the right turned his binoculars on Videl for a brief moment before concentrating once more on the road to Geneva, which entered the square down the side of the main hotel. Videl was fussing with the door of his car, examining the lock, snapping the catch up and down, waiting for the watcher in the van to give him the signal. He heard the engine of a car coming into the square and saw the sidelights of the van come on. He straightened up and began to walk into the café.

'Hell, Jim, watch it!' Evelyn was startled as he was flung against Tassie. Rigbey was swinging the car round in front of the hotel. Instead of stopping in their usual parking place he continued round the side of the hotel and drew up in a narrow alley.

'What is it, Jim?' Evelyn was fully alert and he could feel Tassie tense beside him in the back of the car.

'That was Videl. Going into the café opposite the hotel.'

'Description?'

'Fawn leather hip-length coat, cord trousers. Five foot ten, brown hair, grey at the sides and thin lined face.'

'Stake-out and follow?'

'Yes – Tassie, get your car and take it round the far side of the square. There is plenty of space, so pull up three cars back. He's using a Renault TS16 – one of the square-backed jobs – light coloured, fawn or beige. Mark will meet you when you park. We'll do a passing job when we follow. Standard signalling – OK?'

'OK, Jim.'

Rigbey let the other two out of the car then drove slowly down the alley and out into the next main street. He did a right turn, then another and came back into the main square and parked on the side, at right angles to the café. He saw the Citroën come creeping up across the square and saw Evelyn move across to it and get in.

Videl watched the door of the café. He drank the bitter *café noir* and waited. In the Coq d'Or the man at the first-floor window drew the curtains back sharply and the bearded youth, who had been sitting on his scooter by the café door, climbed slowly off and went inside.

Videl put down his cup and dropped three francs on the counter. He looked down at himself, straightening his jacket as he went out into the street, anything rather than look round for the people who were waiting for him. He could feel the sweat forming under his leather jacket. They would be the hard men out there. Men who would make him talk, if they got their hands on him. Men who would do unmentionable things, and he had to lead them away – out in front – with them panting at his heels. He opened the door of his car and felt a wave of relief as he slammed the door, feeling its tenuous protection.

He coughed twice, clearing the nervousness from his throat, before starting the engine. A Mercedes pulled out from a side street and set off steadily towards Geneva. Keep right behind it, they had said. Don't overtake. They are your protection. He took off the handbrake and followed.

There was little traffic on the road. Monday was not a great night for travelling and it was not difficult to follow the Mercedes. Behind him Videl could see the lights of the cars that had followed him. One of them was closing up. There was a dip – full beam – dip and then the car immediately behind was overtaken and a Citroën came squeezing in between him and the car in front. Another moment and it was off again, overtaking the Mercedes. That would be the first switch. There would be another car still behind him.

Twice during the journey the switch occurred. Once he saw the Citroën parked in a layby and, just before Geneva, he saw the other car for the first time. It was a Ford Granada, with one person in it. Videl nodded to himself. They were good. If he hadn't known they were following he wouldn't have picked them up. There was a short check at the border, then he began to run through the outskirts of the great Swiss city.

The place had been well chosen. It was in the old part of the town, near the lake – an ancient alleyway with cobbled street and sharp-roofed houses on either side. It was a minor tourist spot in summer and there were a couple of bars, a café and a sex shop, most of them excellent sites for keeping watch.

Tassie was driving the lead car and she paused at the entrance to the alley. Evelyn's voice was urgent.

'Go on. This looks like it.'

She drove another block and searched for parking.

'Let me out!'

She stopped and Evelyn got out and walked back towards the Granada. He leant through the window.

'It looks like here. Carry on and park. I'll keep watch.'

Evelyn watched Videl lock his car and open a door by a shop front. There was a bar and a café almost opposite. Evelyn chose the bar. It was easier to get out of in a hurry.

He waited ten minutes before the others joined him.

'Bloody parking in this city is just impossible.' Tassie was brushing her hair back, her face reddened with exasperation.

'No matter, nothing has happened yet. It's across the road.'

Rigbey looked out of the window at the old building opposite.

'What do you think?'

'It's difficult. Big cities are not the best places to keep a prisoner. But then there are bars on the windows and ... Well. It looks right, doesn't it?'

'Not so difficult, drugs, an ambulance and there you are. More difficult to find.'

Tassie shook her head and was about to argue when she grabbed at Rigbey's arm.

'Look – quick. Second floor – window on the right!'

There was the dim outline of a woman wearing a white roll-top sweater. She was standing at the window, holding the curtains back. As they watched she jerked away and the curtains were closed.

They looked at each other.

'Was it, Jim?'

Rigbey was uncertain. He was still staring intently at the window. He spoke slowly.

'I don't know . . . You see . . . well . . . I know this girl rather well and I'm not sure. The clothes are right but . . . well . . . Hell, I'm not sure. The movements weren't right.'

Evelyn looked at him with speculation in his eye.

'Perhaps a come-on?'

'Perhaps. But we can't neglect it. One thing *is* certain. We've got Videl and we'll take him tomorrow and tear the guts out of him until he spews it all up.' He glanced at Tassie. 'You can look the other way, if you're squeamish.'

She smiled grimly.

Rigbey drained his glass.

'I'm going out to look around the place. There should be a room we can take. We'll need it when we operate on Videl.'

He got up to go, then sat down.

'Look slowly, there's an ambulance coming up the road.'

They watched the ambulance stop outside the house across the road.

'Right, Tassie, get back to the car and have the engine running.'

The girl got up and left.

The two ambulance men had entered the house. Two

minutes later they returned carrying a stretcher with a body on it.

'This looks like it. Hurry up, Tassie. We need you.' Rigbey's hands were clenching. The ambulance began to move off.

The door of the bar burst open and Tassie appeared, red in the face. She held out her hand imploringly.

'Keys! Keys! For *your* car! There's a damned great truck double-parked by the Citroën. I can't get it out. Come on, man!'

They left at a run and tore up the alleyway to the main road. Rigbey fumbled open the door of the Granada and they piled in. He pulled out into the road and there was the crunch of broken glass as a car coming from the other direction caught the back of a bicycle and tipped its rider in front of them. Rigbey stood on the brakes and stopped just in time. A crowd was gathering and there was no chance of catching the ambulance now. Rigbey stared at the others and slowly shook his head.

.　　.　　.　　.　　.

It was late on the Monday night and in their house in Champbiére Mme Beyer wished to go to sleep but her husband was pacing the bedroom floor, smoking a rare cigarette. She turned impatiently in the bed.

Beyer made up his mind. She was probably miles away but it was worth a try. He stubbed out the cigarette and picked up the bedside phone.

The call was answered from the barracks immediately.

'Certainly, monsieur. Raoul and Franz. At once, monsieur.'

It was Raoul who answered and he was polite but startled.

'But yes, monsieur, yes indeed. We will start before dawn. You will authorize the vehicle from the car pool?' He hesitated, then went on. 'But, monsieur, why are we not to tell the station sergeant?'

Beyer curled his lip. 'Because, my young friend, there are powerful influences at work. But remember, it is I who recommends for promotion.'

He put the phone down, greatly relieved. After all it was only a routine patrol to check no one was stranded in the snow — all four inches of it. Enough for skis, though, and those two lads were just about the best there were on skis.

9

Tassie Hardwicke sat cross-legged on the bed balancing a bowl of coffee on her legs. Her blonde hair hung loose round her shoulders. She dipped a piece of bread in the coffee and turned her face up to catch the soggy end before it broke away.

Mark Evelyn sat in a chair by the window and watched her and wondered what she would be like in a fight. There was toughness but she had been put out in Geneva when things had gone wrong and had been on the verge of pouting petulance on the way back to Champbiére.

They had reported failure and instructions had been to wait while heavies in the Geneva office put a trace out on the ambulance and Videl's car. It was police work now and the Swiss would co-operate so long as their own nationals weren't involved. They were to move up to Geneva, once a lead had been established.

There was a knock and Rigbey came into the room. He was dressed and he yawned as Evelyn poured coffee for him.

He was still yawning at eleven o'clock when he strolled round the square. Inspector Beyer was standing outside the town hall, standing in the typical policeman's stance, hands clasped behind his back staring into space, looking at nothing, seeing everything.

Rigbey walked towards him. He knew he had been seen but the inspector continued to look in front of him.

'Good morning, Inspector.'

'Good morning, monsieur.'

'It goes well?'

'It goes badly, monsieur.' The inspector's lips were hardly moving. 'Sometimes, you understand, it is difficult for a policeman. No doubt you find the same in your country.' He took a slow look round the square.

'Monsieur, two of my young men happened to be making a routine patrol in the mountains this morning.' He paused and Rigbey felt his mouth go dry. There was something coming.

'Monsieur, there is a mountain hut high up a side valley some four kilometres from Pecheur's house. One would recognize the valley because there is a bridge with a broken handrail on the road immediately before the track that leads up to the hut. My young men say they think the hut is occupied. You understand, monsieur, the information I give you is probably – almost certainly – valueless . . . and please move slowly, not urgently, when you leave me.'

74

'Thanks, Inspector.'

The inspector gave a bare nod and continued to stare at the far side of the square as Rigbey walked slowly back to the hotel. He found the other two in their room and there was a scramble to get into operational clothes as he spoke.

Rigbey talked as they dressed.

'We take everything up to Pierre's house. I still have the room and I know the niece. From there we move out on foot at dusk and make a strike soon after dark.'

'If it's them.'

'Yes, if it's them. But it fits, you know. Think hard about Geneva. Won't London be pleased, if we don't have to deal with the French?' He rolled his eyes as he pulled the sweater over his head.

·   ·   ·   ·   ·

High in the mountains the girl groaned as she rolled off the bed. It felt as though her clothes were sticking to her body. The agony had gone now but there was still a burning sensation and some of the bruises went deep. Videl had been thorough, but it had been a mechanical thoroughness. There had been none of the lip-licking satisfaction her husband had enjoyed and she wondered again about Videl. But he was gone now and she had to think.

She sat on the edge of the bed, hands clasped between her knees. All day she had feigned vomiting attacks, drinking salt water when she went out to the privy or the back of the hut. It had kept Beppo at bay and had left her pale and weak.

It had to be tonight. She couldn't rely on Videl being away another day. Tonight she had to be away . . . or dead. She dug her fingernails into the palms of her hands. Beppo would be her victim. He was vulnerable. She had watched him carefully and he would not be able to control himself. Slowly she got to her feet and untangled the chain. She saw Beppo's hopeful look as she shuffled into the living room.

She went out through the back door once more. Videl's sponge bag was still there. She snatched it up and went into the privy. She unzipped the solid bottom and gave a sigh of satisfaction.

She had been right. There were two disposable syringes in plastic boxes. They were pre-charged. She took one of the boxes and thrust it into the waistband of her skirt, covering it with her sweater. Only Beppo looked up as she went back into the hut.

Beppo sensed something different about the girl. He looked her up and down. Her feet were filthy, toes blackened and ankles grimed. There was a trickle of dried blood from one of the anklets and her bare legs had a dull grubby look. Her hair was in rat-tails and her face sallow and drawn. But there was definitely something different about her. It was the look on her face – a smug, almost self-satisfied look – and then the great eyes were turned on him and the mouth pouted up, lips plump and inviting.

He glanced quickly at Vosper. He was leaning back in his chair with his feet on the table, reading a maga-zine. He looked again at the girl. Her vomiting over the last few hours had dispelled even his urges but she looked better now, more animation. Beppo licked his lips. *Could* that be an invitation in her eyes?

He got up and walked nervously towards her. She stood waiting for him and allowed him to come up close. He could smell her. They all stank but hers was a female smell, a smell of warmth and softness, the smell of moist breasts and other things. Beppo felt the agony starting in his groin.

Slowly he reached out a hand and touched her arm. She did not draw back but merely dropped her eyes and raised them again. She glanced over his shoulder and looked meaningly at Vosper. Beppo felt his throat go dry and tried to breathe normally, but there was not enough air. He nodded briefly and turned to Vosper as the girl moved away into the bedroom.

He could hardly get the words out.

'Vosper, my friend. Would you not wish a little walk? Just for half an hour?' His voice was a husky rasp.

Vosper looked up and his pale lips twisted into a thin smile.

'Got the urge, have you, Beppo? Balls are burning holes in your pants, are they?' He glanced down and sniggered.

'Looks like a flagpole you've got stuck in there. You'll split your seams, if you're not careful.'

Beppo was imploring.

'Vosper, my friend. Just half an hour.'

'It's cold out there.'

'You can take my coat.'

'I like it here.'

'Vosper. I'm bursting, man. She's on heat, I tell you. Go! Please go!'

'You can force her while I'm here. I'll watch.'

'I don't *want* to force her if she's willing. Go, please go. A walk down to the road and back. No more! I tell you Videl's tamed her.'

'A thousand francs?'

'French?'

'Yes.'

'Done.' Beppo let his breath out in a sigh of relief.

Vosper got up slowly and tossed the magazine on the table. He was grinning as he pulled on his quilted jacket.

'I'd laugh if she gave you a dose. You can never tell with these high-class tarts. That husband of hers was clapped to the eyebrows.'

Beppo was impatient, willing him to go. The ribaldry had no effect on him. He could think only of his urgent need.

Vosper made a final joke as he opened the door.

'Watch she doesn't get her legs round your neck and strangle you.'

Beppo started and held out a restraining hand.

'The keys, Vosper. The keys . . . I won't be able to . . . with that chain.'

Vosper's eyes narrowed and there was a wary look on his face.

'I don't like that, Beppo. Can't you . . . ?'

'No!' Beppo's voice rose to a shout. 'No, I can't, I want to do it properly. I *can't* I tell you. I've got to have that key. You'll be down there and, anyway, when I've finished with her, she won't be fit for running. Vosper, I tell you Videl has her down. She'll do anything to please us. I *tell* you, Vosper.'

Vosper drew the keys from his pocket and tossed them to Beppo. His hands jerked out to catch them but the keys fell on the floor. Beppo dropped to his knees, scrabbling with his fingers. Vosper sneered as he went out of the door.

Beppo took several deep breaths and tried to walk steadily towards the bedroom, but his legs were shaking and he felt as though he was going to faint. He reached up and undid another button of his shirt, then turned the door handle.

The girl watched him come into the room. She was lying on the bed with her skirt rucked half-way up her thighs. She had raised herself on her elbows and looked carefully to see if he had the keys. The man was sweating, his hands clenching and unclenching. She let her fingers stray to the edge of the mattress. She could feel the syringe concealed between the edge of the mattress and the wall. She stretched out her legs and offered him her ankles.

Beppo had to make three attempts before he could get the key into the hole. The second lock was easier and he unsnapped the anklets.

The girl felt a wave of pure pleasure flow over her as she felt the galling weight of the chains fall away. She wriggled her feet and settled back on the bed.

He was on her immediately, body half across hers, hands groping furiously at her breasts. She put her hands on his shoulders and pushed gently.

'Softly, my friend. There is plenty of time!'

She felt the pressure of his body ease and he was staring down at her. She pushed again and he drew away. Slowly, her eyes never leaving his, she reached down and slipped her hands up her skirt feeling for the elastic of her pants. She could hear his breath rasping as she pulled down the grubby material. She wriggled her hips to get them over her buttocks then leaned forward to slide them down her thighs and calves and over her feet. She dropped them on the floor and lay back.

He started towards her again but she shook her head. He had to be screaming for it, oblivious to everything else but his bodily anguish. She sat up on the bed and crossed her arms, peeling her sweater up over her breasts. She no longer had a brassière, Videl had torn that off when he had . . . when he had hurt her. She paused for a moment as her nipples came into view, bouncing gently and quivering as the edge of the heavy wool first pressed then released them. Beppo began to whimper and clutched himself, kneading and squeezing. She dragged the sweater over her head and let it fall against the wall, covering the syringe. She gestured with her hands. He must undress.

He tore at buttons, snapping them off and staggered and tripped, almost falling in his eagerness to get his clothes off. He had a thick mat of black curling hair on his chest and a bulging pot belly. He was wildly in-congruous as he hopped, naked except for black nylon socks heavily patterned at the sides and his ponce's shoes. He dragged them off and turned towards her. She closed her eyes and choked back a sob.

He was on her now and she thrust forward to meet him, twisting and tearing at him with her hands, as the pain stabbed through her belly. She writhed against him feeling only terror and hurt. Then her inner conscious-ness asserted itself and the pain subsided as she watched his face. His eyes were glazed and he whim-pered and grunted as he drove himself into her. She bit at his shoulder and he moaned aloud with pleasure. She reached down and raked with her fingernails at his buttocks. He jerked in a spasm and almost ejaculated but caught himself back. She dug her nails into his skin, eight ragged points of sharpness. He groaned again, then gathered her shoulders, pulling her to him. She reached out her hands and groped with her fingers for the syringe. He jerked again and almost rolled from her. She felt her heart lurch in horror as she heard the crunch of breaking plastic and felt terror crowding in on her. She pressed against him, moving in time with him, urging him on to his climax. She wrapped her legs round his thighs, restricting his movement, holding him close to her. He began to shout as he went into his orgasm. She groped for the syringe. She felt the damp patch against the blankets then the sharp edge of the broken barrel and despair came over her in a wave of nausea. She jerked her head sideways looking round the room. There was just one thing that might do. He drew away from her and rolled over on to his side. His eyes were closed and he was breathing in heaving gasps.

She eased herself away from him and swung her legs to the floor. He paid no attention. She got up from the bed and crept towards the door. The broom was leaning against the wall. She gave one frightened glance over her shoulder before snatching it up and swinging round. She had the handle in both hands and she raised it like a sledge-hammer; it cracked against the ceiling. Beppo grunted and began to roll over on the bed as she struck, sobbing with the effort.

At the last moment he saw it coming and fear and shock leapt into his eyes. He tried to get his hands up to protect himself and jerked his head back. The head of the broom struck through the protecting hands and the end of the broom head smashed against his cheekbone, just below the eye.

He screamed, but it was pain and fury, not the agony of a disabled man. He started up from the bed and she turned and fled. She heard the thump of his bare feet as they hit the floor then the swift pad of the footsteps coming after her. She was through the door, running, naked except for her skirt, breasts swinging and hips rippling with tension. Her lowest level of consciousness flashed upon her and she turned as she got through the door into the living room, flattening herself against the wall. Beppo burst through the opening and she stuck out her leg, tripping him, sending him in a headlong dive towards the stove.

He tried to save himself with his hands but his head struck the concrete base of the stove and he cried out only once before rolling over on the wooden floor, dazed and bloody.

Juliette was already running towards the back of the hut. Her hands were trembling with effort as she fumbled at the zip of the wet pack. She broke open the last plastic box and ran fearfully back into the room. Beppo was beginning to lift himself on to his knees.

Now! It had to be *now*!

She flung herself on him, pressing him down under her body — two naked people grotesquely entwined. He slumped under her and she stabbed at his thigh, driving the needle deep, pressing furiously at the plunger. He jerked convulsively and she felt the needle snap.

She pushed away from him, backing in a crouch across the floor as he started to crawl towards her. Foam had appeared on his lips and his eyes were murder. She felt the table behind her and reached back dragging herself upright. He made one last effort and got to his feet facing her. He was swaying. He took one step, then crumpled to the floor.

The tears started now, pouring down her cheeks as she ran back into the bedroom, snatching up her pants, hopping desperately as she pulled them on, then the sweater. She dragged one of the blankets from the bed and flung it round her shoulders. Vosper had been gone fifteen minutes and there was no time for anything else. She ran barefooted to the door, then changed her mind and scurried to the back door, nervously skirting Beppo's supine body. As she stepped off the flagstones into the snow she drew in her breath with the shock of the cold. She crept round the house.

.   .   .   .   .

The strike group had still been bunched together, still too far from the hut for an attack formation, when they heard the footsteps slithering and stumbling towards them. There was no need for the pressure of Rigbey's hands on their shoulders. They all froze into cover at the side of the wide mouth of the valley.

They heard the man curse as he slipped and fell heavily. He cursed in German. Then he was up again and passing them, walking carefully, picking his steps, without urgency; the walk of a man who was feeling the cold but nothing more.

They waited until the sounds faded towards the road. Mark Evelyn spoke first.

'Recognize him?'

'No, not one I know. But one less, if this is the right place. Spread out now. I'll lead.'

Virtually invisible in their snow smocks they adopted their arrow-head formation, moving silently through the whiteness towards the head of the valley. The ground became steeper and the two on the flanks closed in towards the path that ran by the stream. They had been moving for no more than ten minutes when Rigbey stopped then moved swiftly to his right, joining Tassie while Evelyn crouched in a rocky crevice on the left. There was no noise but they had all seen the dark figure running silently towards them.

Juliette Montague could no longer feel the sharpness

of the stones or the cold. Her feet were totally numb and she left bloody footprints as she ran and slipped. The half-moon reflected from the snow, setting off every bush and rock as a patch of deep shadow. The rivulet took a sharp turn in her path and she faltered, seeking a place to jump. There was a rustle and the sudden sensation of a presence on her left, then arms were round her and she was flung to the ground. A hand was over her mouth, choking off the scream of desperate despair and a body was on top of her pressing her into the snow. She shook her head trying to free herself from the hand. There was a voice whispering urgently into her ear.

'It's all right, it's all right. We won't harm you. It's all right. I *promise* you, it's all right.'

It was the smell that brought her out of her terror. She knew the smell. It was a compound of expensive female body lotion and deodorant spray. She had used similar things herself. She stared up at the face pressed close to hers and took in the words. It was a broad face, a woman's face, and blonde hair showed beneath the rim of the hood.

Tassie felt the girl relaxing and she whispered even more urgently. This time turning her head.

'It's her, Jim. Over here, quick!'

Juliette's face crumpled, the high cheek-bones standing out, the mouth twisting beneath and the chin puckering into wrinkles as she wept. She held out her arms to Rigbey as Tassie moved away and he took her place. He held her close for a moment and kissed her cheek.

'How bad is it, my lovely?'

Her tears increased and she laughed bitterly.

'I'm not lovely at all – but it's not too bad. My feet

and ankles hurt and I've been bruised a bit but I can walk.'

'No, you can't. We'll carry you. You would get frostbite, if you tried. How many in the hut?'

'Only one and he's unconscious.'

'Unconscious?' Rigbey's voice rose in query.

'Yes. But there's another. He went for a walk while Beppo was . . . was . . . Well, he just went for a walk and he'll be coming back.'

He felt the tension of fear in her body.

'Never mind him, my love. There were just the two?'

'Those two and Videl, but he's away, right away, just now.'

'Fine, my darling. Now . . . !' He rose to his knees and scooped her up in his arms. 'Light as a feather. They can't have been feeding you well. Mark and I will take it in turns. Tassie!'

'Yes, Jim.'

'Out in front, please, and take the other man.' Then to Juliette, 'What's his name?'

'Vosper. He's a German.'

'Right, Tassie. Take Vosper. No need to be gentle. We'll give you two minutes.'

She melted away into the moonlight and the three of them waited, the girl clutching tightly to the man who was holding her.

10

The director had assembled an audience for his phone call. Mealie Jimmy had declined the invitation but a man from the Prime Minister's office had come as quickly as a police car could bring him. Jones was there and Sarah Hardinge was standing watch over the tape recorder. The director smiled, thinly, as he waited for the French switchboard operator to connect him. They saw him come alert.

'Ah! Glasiére, my dear fellow. So sorry to trouble you so late at night . . . What? Is it really that time in Paris . . . I'm sorry, I had forgotten the time difference. However, this is most important. We need the help of your infiltrator before he abandons his post. It is absolutely vital that we know if there is a Wolf pack operating in England.'

He paused and listened for a moment. The others could see Sarah Hardinge smiling between her headphones.

'Yes, Glasiére, I appreciate you would not wish to imperil him just before he departs but we have good news for you on that front. He needn't go!'

There was a long pause, the receiver squawked. The director held the telephone an inch away from his ear. Finally he spoke again.

'I *had* thought you would be delighted, my dear fellow. The girl is quite safe and we intend to look after her. A little damaged but nothing that time won't cure.' He paused, frowning slightly in polite puzzlement.

'But, Glasiére, you gave us a week and your man has not been delivered up to the Wolves . . . Very well, I will ask the Prime Minister's representative. He is here with me.' He looked enquiringly at the man from the Prime Minister's office, who shook his head.

'No, I'm sorry. The Prime Minister is quite firm. There can be no deal. We have played our part.' His

86

voice became cold. 'By all means take it to the highest level. I have already consulted mine.'

He put the phone down and looked at the Prime Minister's representative.

'Just in case you think we are being less than generous, we understand that Glasiére ordered his men not to assist us in the search for the girl.'

The other man looked sick for a moment before he lowered his eyes.

In Paris, Glasiére was raging. Never, *never*, trust the British. His old uncle, who had fought at Verdun, had told him that as a child and he cursed himself for forgetting the advice. He picked up the phone and swore once again at the operator, who was trying to raise Manet.

.   .   .   .   .

Inspector Beyer heard the news of the rescue just before midnight. He put out a general alarm and police had driven straight to the hut. They found Vosper on the way up and stared in wonder at his condition, but Beppo had gone. Still, they had a good description and he wouldn't get far. Vosper screamed and fainted as they lifted him on to the stretcher.

The police activity had not gone unnoticed and Streicher was woken from his sleep. He ordered a cautious reconnaissance and a young German took his car and skis up the road. He passed the mouth of the valley and travelled another two kilometres before stopping and ski-ing back. What he saw sent him flying to his vehicle and the nearest telephone.

Beyer stayed in the Gendarmerie for the rest of the night, listening to the reports coming in over the radio. He had seen the girl and knew her condition. At four he heard the latest news on Vosper. He had been taken to Chamonix and the doctors had nodded over his visible condition. When they had cut the clothes off him they had stared hard, then rushed him to the X-ray room. The plates were still wet when they ordered the theatre to be prepared for an emergency operation.

At six-thirty, an hour before dawn, a patrol car spotted Beppo. He was on foot and was trying to get a lift towards Switzerland.

Beyer hitched himself off the table where he had been sitting and gave orders that he was to be observed but not disturbed. A second car was to move up on the far side but he, Beyer, would make the arrest, and he would make it alone.

He left the radio room and went back into his office. He unlocked a cupboard and selected an item of equipment he had not used since the bad old days of 1968. He went out to his car.

The patrol car was easy to see. He slowed down and called through the window.

'Yes, monsieur, he is still there. We have been stopping all cars and warning them not to pick him up.'

Beyer nodded and wound his window up. The men in the patrol car looked at each other questioningly and wondered at the expression on his face. He found Beppo in a lay-by, a kilometre down the road. The fat Italian started forward eagerly as the car slowed down, then turned and began to run as he saw the peaked kepi. He heard the slam of the car door as Beyer came after him, the rubber-soled footsteps crunching the gravel.

Beppo fled down the woodland path that led from the lay-by. Within a minute he was exhausted and he could feel the policeman at his shoulder, hear his

88

panting breath. He slithered to a stop and turned and stared in astonishment. There was no gun, only a riot baton which the policeman was tapping in the palm of his left hand.

Beppo felt a surge of hope. This he could deal with. He reached for the knife at his hip, pressing the button that released the blade. Eight inches of handle and seven inches of steel, no thicker than a rapier. He went down into a crouch, left arm back, right almost fully stretched before him, point low, ready for a double-ment.

Beyer took a step forward, arm half-bent, the riot stick at an angle across his body. The little bastard would go for his wrist. Right! Let's tempt him! He took another step and extended his arm, stick pointed forward.

Beppo leapt, arm going down, point angling upwards for the slash at wrist that would sever the great artery and disable his opponent. Beyer stayed where he was but his wrist arched up and the riot stick swept round in a curve striking Beppo's wrist bone, numbing the nerves and sending the knife flashing in the early morning light to fall in the grass of the verge.

'Now! my friend!' Beyer struck hard for the solar plexus. Beppo doubled up in pain and the baton struck him behind the ear. He fell to the ground, gasping for breath. Beyer stood above him and swept his arm up high. Beppo had never known such pain, never believed it could be possible.

It was a wholly illegal weapon Beyer was using. It was made of hard rubber and it could beat a man into insensibility without leaving the telltale bruises and scars that so excited the liberal press. For two whole minutes he used this instrument on the Italian, pound-

89

ing his muscles almost into jelly. He stopped only when Beppo was a quivering mass of obese flesh. He turned and walked slowly back to his car radio.

II

It had been a fine-run thing. Claude Manet had ignored Glasiére's furious calls from French security headquarters. He had been packing his grip, destroying anything that might give an inkling of where he was going. Every ten minutes the phone would burst into shrill life and go on ringing for a full twenty double rings before it cut off. Once, just as Manet scooped up his grip, tucking it under his arm while he switched off the lights and fumbled with the lock of his apartment door, the phone rang again. This time it was only two minutes since the last call and the phone rang exactly ten times before it stopped, but by then Manet had gone.

Out in the Ninth Arrondissement a leading member of the Paris Wolf pack put down the phone with a puzzled frown. It was almost the hour for communication and the pack leader should have been available. Probably in the loo. He would ring again in ten minutes. But in ten minutes' time Manet was already in his car, fighting his way through the late-night traffic.

Manet was fleeing for his life. He travelled southeastwards from Paris, picking up the great trunk road at Dijon and then south to Bandol which lay on the coast between Marseilles and Toulon. He felt the touch of fear every time lights appeared in his mirror. Had he known that two hours after he had left three members of the Paris pack had visited his apartment to learn why the council member was not answering his phone, his fear would have turned to terror.

It had taken them an hour to make sure, searching the apartment and garages and, finally, phoning the contact number in Basel who, in turn, phoned Geneva. For the past fifty minutes orders had been flowing out of the operations room in Switzerland and all over south-western Europe the Wolves were awake and on the prowl. When Geneva heard the news of the girl's rescue they would be turned into a slavering horde.

Manet was making good time. Except for petrol and the lavatory, he had driven non-stop for eight hours. The fear was beginning to leave him. Eight hours is a long time to be continually afraid and, as each potential hazard receded, each moment of terror was proved craven, he began to take courage and to believe that he would make it after all.

There was a watery sun above the horizon when he swung off the highway into Avignon. He had to have coffee and food. It was at that moment that he was spotted. Every highway out of Paris had its watchers, as did every major port and airfield. He had been lucky and the first ring at Auxerre had missed him, but the boy and girl lying in their tent by the side of the Route Nationale, outside Avignon, picked him up in their binoculars from a kilometre away.

From there onwards Manet was never without a shadow. The word went out and cars converged on the main route. Others fanned out from Marseilles, while the killer squad began its preparations. As Manet took the bypass of the great seaport, he had two cars in front and one behind, manned from three different Wolf packs.

It was ten o'clock when he ran into Bandol. In summer the town is crowded with French holidaymakers and the beaches are aquiver with bare-breasted female sunbathers. In early winter the residents have the place to themselves and the small-boat harbour is full of sheeted craft laid up for the season, while only the multi-coloured fishing boats and a few of the others still used the harbour. Graugin's boat was one of the others. It was twelve metres – nearly forty feet – and it could cross the Mediterranean with ease.

Manet parked his car two streets away from the old harbour. He got out and stretched, arms out wide. He yawned. He felt as though he had been driving for ever. He locked the car and walked towards the harbour. It was ten-fifteen and the killer squad had just left Marseilles.

Manet strolled along the quai. The sun had strengthened and the clouds rolled away to give a hard bright Riviera winter sky. The waterfront was a jumble of cafés, restaurants, boat agencies and ships' chandlers. He would find Graugin in a bar at the far end, the Au Bon Coin.

It was a cut above the other places and the two tarts, who were sitting over their cassis, looked smart and even faintly pretty. Manet walked up to the bar and ordered a pression. He looked round the bar. There was no danger, just a couple arguing quietly in the corner and a young fellow in a denim suit reading a newspaper. One of the tarts glanced up at him speculatively. He gave her a neutral smile and a slight shake of the head. She smiled back, no offence taken, and turned again to her companion.

He waited half an hour and drank another beer before leaving the bar, walking slowly back up the quai. He knew the name of the boat and he spotted it almost immediately – a heavy job but one that would take anything.

There was no sign of Graugin. He had hoped they could have sailed immediately but he had been told from six each evening, that was the guarantee. He had not taken into account this panic. His plan had been to sleep on the way but his fear had driven him on. He stared around. There was nothing unusual. Bandol was as safe a place as any.

At this moment the killer squad was only twenty kilometres away. There were three of them, all men. There was no talking in the car. The driver kept licking his lower lip as he drove.

Manet stood looking at the boats. He would have to do something between now and six. He thought of a cinema, but that was a public place and meant going back into the town. There was the girl, of course. He turned and walked back to the Au Bon Coin.

The two women were still there. The one who had smiled at him looked up questioningly as he came back into the bar. He went to their table.

She had blonde hair that had been bleached so often that it had taken on a dry, straw colour. She had good teeth when she smiled. She moved her chair to make room for him.

He bowed politely to the other girl, who was collecting her things together. She got up with a sideways twist of her hips and smiled knowingly to her companion as she left.

Manet sat down at the table and met the girl's gaze. There was no questioning look now. It was only a question of the price. He had never bought sex before – never had to – but he felt no embarrassment. She was on the plump side, about thirty – wide mouth, overfull with teeth – and she kept dabbing at her hair with her hand.

'You are free?'

She smiled.

'I'm not occupied but I'm certainly not free.'

He grinned at her impudence.

'How much?'

'Just the ordinary? Nothing special?'

'Just the ordinary.'

'One hundred francs.'

He was surprised at the cheapness.

'How long is that for?'

'Half an hour, unless you're a superman.'

'How much for the afternoon – until six?'

She stopped to consider. There would be no trade until the evening anyway. She shrugged.

'Three hundred francs.' She looked at him questioningly. 'Lonely, are you?'

He smiled grimly and stood up. 'You have a place nearby?' She nodded. She was slipping the handle of her bag over her arm as she rose from her chair. She had good legs and a good behind. As they walked down the quai, they were observed from three different angles. The Wolves had gathered in a tight ring.

The tart's place was a small room at the top of a flight of uncarpeted stairs. There was a double bed and a dressing table with cracked veneer and a green stained mirror. He stood and watched her as she unbuttoned her dress. She had big breasts and they fell forward as she pulled the garment over her head.

.   .   .   .   .

94

The killer squad was travelling with full equipment. Normally an assassination was carefully planned and carefully timed. The weapons were pre-selected and the get-away covered every eventuality. This time it was different. They would have to improvise – take the opportunities as they came. They had come with everything they might need. The driver pulled up gently in a small square, some distance from the waterfront. As he got out of the car a couple of girls strolled up. Their intelligent faces belied their sluttish clothes.

'He's waiting for something. There's a boat he's interested in. We'll know who owns it in another half-hour. But there's no activity yet. He's picked up a girl. She's a known professional and they're in her room now.'

'How long?'

'Fifteen minutes.'

The driver thought for a moment. Half an hour was usual for a trick. But the man was obviously waiting. You don't drive like a maniac through the night just to pick up a prostitute. The man must be early for his rendezvous. He nodded.

'Get back and keep watch – keep us under observation too.'

He was a medium man. Medium height, medium colouring, medium clothes. He had a round face, a clerk's face, until you looked at the eyes and then you thought of the religious fanatics of the Middle Ages. The two men with him had been carefully chosen, originally as much for their nondescript appearance as for their potential as killers but their training had been thorough and complete. The three of them sat in the car. They were called Opal One, Two and Three. Opal Three spoke.

'We could go in and kill them both.'

Opal One shook his head. 'It's got to be spectacular. This is an execution. The word has got to get back. The boat will be better, once we're sure.'

'Suppose he finishes with the tart.'

'I think it will be a long job. Anyway, we will look. Three stays here with the kit. Two comes with me.'

The two men walked slowly towards the seafront. As they did so, a young man sitting outside a café began to mutter to himself. He was actually speaking into a microphone hung round his neck and clipped to the lapel of his jacket. Within two minutes the message had been relayed via Basel to Geneva and noted in the operations room.

Opal One stared at the boat. He smiled at the name painted on the stern, *The Unicorn's Horn*. It looked big enough to go anywhere in the Mediterranean. A few moments ago he had heard who it belonged to. A man called Graugin – ex-Legionary – ex-revolutionary – ex-mercenary – and presently a smuggler. Opal One noted the layout of the boat, moored stern on to the quai. There was a deep cockpit with door leading to the saloon and a stepped up bridge with spoked wheel and navigational aids. There was a radar scanner mounted above the bridge.

Opal One stood for a long time, thinking. It would all depend on whether they went down into the saloon. If they did it would be spectacular enough, my word it would! He turned slowly and walked carefully round the surrounding area before going back to the car.

Opal Three came alert as he saw the leader approaching and wound down the window. Opal One put his head inside.

'How many incendiaries do we have?'

'Two phosphorous sticks.' Opal Three looked expectantly at Number One.

'Timers?'

'Plenty, both sorts.'

'How many grenades?'

'Five anti-personnel, five high explosive.'

Number One nodded. His memory had been confirmed. He began to give instructions. There would be
other things they would need.

.   .   .   .   .

Manet rolled off the girl for the last time. It had been
his third orgasm. He turned on his side and held his
wrist high above his head, watch downwards. It was
half past five and time to move.

His clothes were scattered over the room. He swung
his legs wearily to the floor. It had been a hard grind.
He collected his things and began to dress slowly.

The girl watched him curiously from the bed. It
hadn't been too bad in the end, she'd actually enjoyed
the last bit, and that wasn't usual when she was doing
a trick. She smiled to herself at his tiredness, the slow
fumbling with the trousers, the blinking eyes, the loose
mouth. Poor sod! He really looked shagged. Her smile
deepened as she thought of a job well done.

Manet took out the money, counting out four hundred francs, watching her smile broaden yet further as
she saw it appearing. He grinned at her as he dropped it
on the dressing table – that was the approved way –
an honorarium, not a payment. He buttoned up his
coat and gave her a wave.

It was sharply cold outside and he put his hands in
his pockets and hunched his shoulders as he trotted
down the steps of the apartment house. As he walked

briskly down the street towards the harbour a flurry of activity broke out behind him.

Support groups had moved up by now and Geneva had approved the operation. Equipment had come in and if a cockroach had made a dangerous move on board *The Unicorn's Horn* it would have been blasted into pulp.

Manet turned the corner on to the quai. There was still no sign of life on board the boat and he went on to the Au Bon Coin. Graugin was sitting at the bar, his great body stretching the sweat shirt and jeans. Graugin never felt the cold. He turned as Manet came into the bar and grinned slowly.

'Claude, my friend. So long – too long.'

He held his right hand out to shake, the left hand out to one side to bring it in on the slap of friendship.

Manet felt his fear slipping away. They had been through much together, the two of them, and always there had been the slow grin, the squeeze of the hand when they met and the fast vicious action when they fought together.

Graugin was pulling him to the bar.

'Come my friend, a drink.'

Manet held back, straining against the persuasive hand. His fear came back in a great gobbet, forcing its way up his throat. He shook his head.

'Can't we just go?'

Graugin's eyes narrowed and he continued the pressure.

'Come, my friend, there are things you must know.'

They sat at the bar. Graugin ordered cognac and leaned towards Manet, speaking softly.

'You seem to have caused some excitement here, my friend. There are many new people in town – ugly people – and they are collecting round the harbour.'

Manet felt the terror prickling down his shoulders and hands.

'How do you know?'

'I am told about these things – the police and Customs usually, but this time much worse. They are perhaps watching the boat and it may be difficult for you to get on board without danger.'

Manet glanced at him sharply. Was Graugin going to let him down? Graugin grinned. He had seen and interpreted the fear.

'My friend, we must be cunning. You will go to the far end of the quai. You will leave here five minutes after me. Walk quickly down the quai. It is about half a kilometre. At the far end where the breakwater nears its end is a flight of steps. Go down them and I will be there. If there is a boat moored, then cross it to reach me. Understood?'

Manet nodded.

'They may try and take you when they see the boat coming in. You must run the last piece.'

Manet nodded again as Graugin heaved himself off the bar stool.

. . . . . .

The killer squad had been active. They had watched Graugin return to his boat, then set off for the bar. Three young men had been keeping observation while Opal One and Opal Three had gone aboard the boat. There had been no difficulty with the saloon door and Opal One had gone swiftly to the bunks that lined the cabin. Under each bunk was a row of drawers, except for the centre bunks where there were cupboards. Opal One pulled open a bottom drawer. It was empty except for three old paperbacks. Opal Three was carrying a satchel. He unclipped the flap and handed Number One two fat sausages of plastic explosive. He reached far inside the drawer and pressed the explosive to the back, then took the two strips of adhesive tape that were passed to him, taping the explosive in position. Delicately he set the grub-screw timer and pressed it on to the detonator which, in turn, went into the explosive. Between them he taped an anti-personnel grenade.

They worked quickly. Opal Two joined them, reporting that Manet had joined Graugin in the bar. More explosive with another grenade was taped under the trap that led to the bilges. Then they were up and moving back into the cockpit. The engine-room hatch was in the stern. Opal One let himself drop down into the cramped compartment and taped an incendiary tube to the main fuel lead and a massive explosive charge under the propeller-shaft housing. As he reappeared on deck a fourth figure was standing there, outlined against the lights of the harbour side.

'Graugin has left the bar.'

The words were softly spoken and all four of them stepped up on to the quai, walking away, hands in pockets, talking and laughing together. The explosives were only a precaution in case the main job went badly wrong.

.　　.　　.　　.　　.

Graugin strolled towards his boat. He was whistling one of the Legion songs and he slow-marched through the quick-time. He saw two figures pressed up against a wall and his muscles tensed until he saw the whiteness of a girl's legs and part of a thigh, where a hand was groping up her skirt. He relaxed slightly, but only slightly. As he passed the couple the man withdrew his hand. The girl wriggled with disappointment – it had been getting interesting and she had felt herself moistening with desire. But the Wolves' business had to come first. The man brought the transistor up to his face and spoke quietly into it.

There was no one in sight near the boat. Graugin stood, staring round into the darkness. He was armed, had been since the whisper came in, and he was prepared to fight. He turned and stepped on board, the boat giving gently under his weight. At the door into the saloon he paused and went down on one knee. He groped in the darkness, feeling for the sellotape he had stuck across the join. He straightened up slowly; it was hanging loose.

Once before in Indo-China he had had the same feeling. It had been a long patrol and the rains had been on. They had splashed back into camp, leaning into the deluge, not caring how they walked. He was past the guardhouse before he realized that there had been no challenge and there had been a whole five seconds of frozen horror as he saw the triangular yellow faces and realized that the safe place, the refuge, was no longer safe. Then the night had opened up and he had forgotten his fear. Even now he could feel the twinging above his right nipple, where the grenade fragment had struck.

He stood looking carefully around him. They would have him in their sights, there would be a rifle aimed at him, cross-hairs on a telescope would be centred on his chest. He swallowed, forcing down the excitement. There must be no unusual movement, nothing to cause the finger to tighten on the trigger.

·   ·   ·   ·   ·

The man behind the telescopic sight eased his finger off the trigger. Opal One lowered the binoculars for a moment. He turned his head briefly to Opal Two.

'I was worried then, but it seems normal now. Manet should join him at any moment. They will want to be ready to go as soon as he is on board.'

The plan was simple, as all improvised plans should be. If Manet and Graugin went down into the saloon there would be a quick rush of figures from the shadows, a grenade would be tossed through the door, an iron bar jammed through the two grip handles and the figures would jump back on to the harbour as the first explosion set off the other taped explosives. There would then be a spectacular fireworks display, which would demonstrate adequately and dreadfully the dangers of betraying the Wolves. If they did not go to the saloon, Manet and Graugin would be shot as they cast off and the boarding party would operate as before. After all, it mattered little if they were dead when it happened.

The transistor held by Opal Three began to crackle. He listened intently, then said:

'Manet is leaving the café.'

They looked at each other and the excitement showed. They heard a boat's engine start up – that would be Graugin, eager to be away. Opal Two tensed, half standing, reaching out and grabbing for Number One's arm.

'The boat's moving! The boat's moving out!'

They crowded to the window. The boat was already twenty metres from the quai and accelerating. Opal One's mind was racing as the other two watched open-mouthed. He turned sharply to Number Three.

'Call them up. Where's Manet?'

There was a brief pause, then . . .

'He's still walking down the quai . . . No he's not, he's running!'

Opal Two brought the rifle up. They could hear the footsteps, through the open window, the urgency pounding at the stones of the quai. Opal One was in an agony of indecision. It had to be spectacular – a warning to all the others. A bullet in the back running along a harbour side would make no more than the local papers; if Opal Two *could* hit a running man by the harbour lights. Then it was too late – the man was past them. Opal One unfroze.

'Come on – after him!' His anger with himself at his own indecision raised his voice to a scream. The three of them went tumbling down the stairs of the warehouse and through the broken door.

Manet had two hundred metres' lead and they would never catch him except . . . except the fool was running out to the ·breakwater and they would have him cornered.

Manet sensed the figures crowding out of the shadows behind him. He ran, knees up, elbows pumping. He could feel the agony of the bullet in his back. The end of the jetty was another fifty metres and he could hear the throaty growl of the boat's engines. He gasped deeply, forcing the air down into his lungs. The boat was only ten metres away as he jumped on to the top step, going down them two at a time. He could see Graugin's face as a white blur peering over the saloon lights. The nose of the boat bumped gently against the bottom step and he leaped, scrabbling with his hands at the low rail. The bows were already swinging away and he lay flat on his belly, waiting for the shots.

·   ·   ·   ·   ·

Opal Two was firing carefully, squeezing the trigger, not pulling, holding his breath as he fired. There was no response from the boat. It just wasn't possible to fire a heavy rifle after running three hundred metres. He leant his shoulder against the lamp standard and fired twice more. There was no result. Number One slapped him on the shoulder. It was time to go – the sirens would be starting up in a moment and the place would be swarming with police.

.   .   .   .   .

Graugin's laugh broke through the shower of spray that came up over the bows.

'So they didn't beat us, my friend!' He pulled at Manet's shoulder. 'Here, take the wheel. See that light out there – double blinks? Keep her a hand's breadth to the right of that.'

'What are you going to do?' Manet was almost numb with relief.

'Just a routine check down below.' Graugin's teeth flashed white in the cockpit light. He opened the door and swung down into the saloon. He began to search methodically, starting at the forward end. It took six minutes to find the explosive and the grenade in the drawer under the bunk. He glanced at the timer setting and whistled between his teeth as he moved swiftly back into the cockpit. There were twelve minutes left to go. He held out the bundle, showing it to Manet before tossing it into the water. He dropped back into the saloon and continued his search, grunting with satisfaction as he completed it. He was about to leave when he turned back and knelt on the decking, prising up the bilge cover. He stared hard at the taped explosive, then ran with the fat sausages and the globular grenade in his hand, hurling them into the sea. He stood for a moment staring back into the wake, then turned and smiled at Manet.

'I really think that was the last of it.'

.   .   .   .   .

The police had found the empty cartridge cases on the quai and were going through the motions of searching the area. Only a sergeant was actually looking out to sea when the charges under the boat's propeller shaft ignited and the explosion came; a quick white flash of heat expanding into a bright patch of red flame, then the thump of the explosion, flat and heavy across the sea. No one saw the fragments of the boat or the bloody pieces of meat as they sprayed into the air before showering down into the water.

12

Wolves have to be fed. If they are not they will turn on their leaders and tear and rend them. If they are not kept active they become dangerous to themselves, snapping and worrying at each other until the pack is torn by dissension. It was the turn of the Munich and Nice packs to have some exercise and to gather in the prey and their prey was a bank in Nice.

In Nice, Cerise Nolan woke to the brassy ring of her alarm clock at seven o'clock, a full three hours before her normal time of waking. At night she worked in a casino, deft hands stacking the chips, flicking the little white ball against the spin of the wheel, eyes missing nothing. In the mornings she slept late, but not this morning. For a moment she lay in the warmth wondering what it was she had to do, then flung back the bedclothes as memory returned.

She slept without clothes, wearing only a key on a fine chain round her neck. The chill of the morning struck at her skin as she walked across to the window and drew back the curtains a few inches. She had trained for the ballet and had a dancer's figure and walk. It was a grey day. There was a fine drizzle and it would be snowing up in the mountains. She shivered and twisted the knob on the radiator, bringing it to maximum, then padded into the bathroom and ran hot water in the tub. She stretched in front of the mirror and pushed the hair away from her face. It was a thin face running smoothly down from the hair line then narrowing rapidly to a pointed chin under a broad mouth. Her hair was naturally jet black and she kept it thick and shoulder length. That way she could vary its style at will. It was an interesting face. But then why shouldn't it be. She was twenty-two and a woman of experience and she was rising fast in the hierarchy of the Wolves.

It took her twenty minutes to finish in the bathroom and she came out, wrapped in a quilted housecoat. She walked barefoot into the kitchen and dropped a handful of beans into the coffee machine, then heated rolls while the coffee was filtering, before walking into her living room with the breakfast tray.

She put the tray on the coffee table and moved to the safe that had been cemented into the corner of the room. She took the key from its chain, unlocked the door and took out a slim bundle of papers.

They were the detailed plans of the bank raid. She already knew them off by heart but she spent half an hour going over them yet again. It was her first time in command and she felt the surge of excitement as she went through the check lists, occasionally leaning forward to take a sip of coffee or chew slowly at a roll.

She bundled the papers together and went back into the bedroom to dress. The Munich team would be well on their way by now.

. . . . .

Johann Walther reached his hand down between his legs and pulled at the crotch of his trousers. They had left at four in the morning and had been driving for six hours and his behind had gone to sleep. They had been training hard, knowing that it was a bank job but not knowing where. Now they knew – Nice – straight there, a quick job and out again. There were six of them. The four men, Diamonds One to Four, and he was Diamond Four and the two girls, Sapphires One and Two. Sapphire One saw his movement and put her hand on his groin, moving it gently up and down. He took her wrist and pushed it away. In the flashing light from the street lamps he saw her grinning at him. Diamond One was driving the second car and Walther could see the lights behind them.

Diamond Three swung the car off the motorway and into the northern suburbs of Nice. There were dull, ordinary houses, none of the glamour of a Riviera resort. Diamond Three was driving slowly, looking for the pick-up point. He jammed on the brakes, making noises of exasperation as he passed the filling station where they were to contact the locals. He pulled into the next side road on the right, turned and went back. Diamond One followed them like a shadow.

As the car was being filled with petrol, a girl came up to the driver's window. She had jet-black hair twisted into a knob at the back of her head. She walked with a lithe dancer's scamper, toes pointed slightly outwards. She spoke in French.

'Where are you from?'

'From Munich.'

'A jewel of a city.'

'Yes, a jewel and we are the Diamonds and Sapphires.'

The girl smiled and leaned forward, resting her elbows on the edge of the car window.

'I prefer a topaz. I'm in the cream Volvo. Follow me.' She pulled her head out of the car and walked back to her own, shoulders hardly moving, legs swinging from the hips, taut rump rippling under her jeans.

It was not difficult to follow her. She waited for them after each intersection and when she was through the lights before them. It was ten fifteen and the operation was due to start at eleven.

.   .   .   .   .

Topaz Three could feel the palms of his hands sweating. Topaz Four was hanging on to his free arm, her fingers driving into his flesh. He slipped his arm round her and pulled her to him, kissing her lightly on the cheek. She was small, hardly five foot two and dark and vibrant. Too nervy, perhaps, for this job. The brown eyes flashed at him appealingly.

'Easy, my girl – easy. We're almost through. This is

the place. Come, my love, we have rehearsed it and now! The opening night! Except it's morning.'

She caught his smile, white teeth flashing in encouragement, and he felt her fingers relax. They were approaching the boutique of one of the lesser department stores of Nice. Topaz Four dropped her hand from her companion's arm and smoothed her fingers down her hips. She could feel her confidence returning. She was committed now and apprehension fell away from her as she went into the act. She ran her hand along a rack of dresses, sending the hangers into clicking movement, the multicoloured clothes swaying and bouncing under the rail. Topaz Four pulled out a black cocktail dress and stood back, holding it up against her, head on one side, looking enquiringly at her man. Topaz Three nodded in approval.

The sales girl, smiling at a prospective commission, was hovering within distance and Topaz Four was swept away to a changing room, a conspiratorial half-wink twinkling back towards the man who would be paying.

Left alone in the curtained cubicle, Topaz Four moved quickly. The sling bag she carried was weighted down with incendiaries and timers. The cubicle was made of hardboard finished off with a plastic vinyl. It was some four feet square and there were heavy velvet curtains and pelmet. She stood on the plush armchair and pushed an incendiary cylinder into the heavy brocade that trimmed off the top of the side curtains. She dragged the chair across the small cubicle and pushed another into the far side. The timers had been pre-set and there was nothing more to do. She dragged off her dress just in time. The sales girl's face was anxious as she peered round the curtain.

'It's all right, I got my zip stuck.'

Down in the hardware section Topaz Three was inspecting the selection of paints. He knelt down on the floor, pulling out a couple of tins. He was in the angle of the wall behind the racks. There was no one nearby. You didn't need assistance to buy paint. The incendiary tube slid gently down his sleeve and clanked only once as it struck a tin. Then he was pushing the paint back round it. He stretched up cautiously as though his back was stiff, looking round him with the air of a man who has to be careful how he moves. There was still no one there. If there had been and he had been questioned he would have thrown the thunderflash smoke bomb that would have cleared the room. Slowly he walked away from the paint and bought a screwdriver and a hammer. Topaz Four joined him at the entrance. She was smiling her relief.

As they walked together out of the store, Topaz Five and Topaz Six were finishing off their job just down the road. They had set their incendiaries in a seven-storeyed office block, widely distributing them in broom cupboards.

.   .   .   .   .

Cerise Nolan parked the Volvo in the public car park within sight of the bank. The other two cars pulled in to widely separated parking spaces. As she got out she noticed with approval the French licence plates. They would do nothing for two minutes to give her time to get to the command post. She had just forty metres to go. It should take her sixty-five seconds – that was what the rehearsals had shown. She had gone no more than ten steps when she heard a shout behind her.

'Hey! Mademoiselle.' It was the voice of authority.

The car-park attendant was surprised at the girl's reaction. Jumped as though he'd shot her. Pretty little piece and looking as scared as hell. Probably off to see her married boy friend and starting at shadows. He pointed to her car door, which had caught only on the first catch. The girl's shoulders came down with relief and then she was running back, actually running, to bang the door shut, then off again at a sprint. Must be some man she was going to see.

Cerise Nolan was counting her steps as she ran. This was what leadership was all about. Coping with things that went wrong. Topaz Two looked at her questioningly as she burst into the room. She shook her head.

'No trouble – small hitch.' She slipped into the chair, put the headphones over her head and took up the binoculars. She moved in her chair so that she could speak into the microphone that stood on its stand.

. . . . .

Diamond One linked his arm in that of Sapphire One. She was wearing a dark wig and she had coloured contact lenses. She was dressed as an affianced girl should be, smartly but soberly. The disguise for this job couldn't be too elaborate but they had painted a red birthmark on her wrist so that it showed beneath the cuff of her coat, well powdered, as if to conceal it. Diamond Two and Sapphire Two counted out the paces. At fifty they got out of their car and followed. Diamond Three clicked his stop watch into action and watched the swinging fingers. He snapped off the mechanism and nodded to Johann Walther.

'OK – Off.' He ducked his head as he got out of the car and whispered into the microphone, concealed in the front of his shirt.

'Diamond Three and Diamond Four moving off.'

In the control room Cerise Nolan ticked off the seventh item on the operational plan and lifted the binoculars again.

Diamond Three and Diamond Four pulled the bundle of skis from the roof of their car. It was early in the season for skis but not totally impossible and no one would give them a second glance. The thermic lance was well concealed and even if it hadn't been there were few people in Nice at five to eleven on a weekday morning who would recognize it for what it was. It was there in case they met a hero and they had to burn their way in.

Diamond One and Sapphire One had entered the door of the bank. They had an appointment with the manager at eleven o'clock. It had been made by telephone the day before – a young couple about to be married and anxious to open an account and, perhaps, later on when they had proved their responsibility the negotiation of an overdraft. The manager had been sympathetic. Sapphire One clung closely to her fiancé's arm and let the excitement sparkle in her eyes. The manager's secretary smiled indulgently. She would learn in time, the little one!

On the first floor of the department store Mme Hachette was trying to squeeze herself into a dress that was a size too small for her. It was always the same – the back and waist would fit perfectly but the hips were just that half centimetre too wide. Ah! well, at forty-two one had to allow for a little discomfort. It was a pity, though, because black had always suited her. She sighed and unzipped the dress, stepping out of it carefully and reaching for its hanger. At that moment there was a slight *phut* as though someone had blown out sharply through pursed lips. It seemed as though it came from the top of the cubicle. She looked up curiously, wondering for a moment if someone was observing her. Because of this she lost the sight of her right eye. There was a tiny explosive charge in the incendiary tube, sufficient to blow the burning contents ten yards. Mme Hachette got the full force of the explosion down the right side of her face.

For a second she was paralysed with fright, then the searing agony as the phosphorous began to eat into her skin and the terror as her nylon slip flashed on fire and the curtains of the cubicle erupted into red flames sent her tumbling out into the shop.

Jean Robert, assistant floor manager, saved her life. He flung himself at her sending her sprawling to the floor, grinding his body on top of the shrieking flesh, rubbing the phosphorous on to the carpet, where it set off swift streams of fire racing outwards towards the curtains.

There was pandemonium. The great glass double-doors that led on to the staircase were jammed with screaming women and white-faced men. One woman went down and the bodies began to pile up over her. Grey smoke billowed out into the staircase and swirled upwards, terrifying the startled customers on the floor above, sending them scampering still higher to escape it.

The senior saleswoman had been through the war and she sat at her desk calmly dialling the emergency number. She heard the tearful voice of one of the switchboard operators – Marie Daudin. She was only a kid and it should have been the supervisor who answered on that number.

'Bomb gone off in ladies' garments, Marie. Put this through to fire and police.'

'Yes, madame.' She heard the girl sob.

'Marie, listen to me, where is the supervisor?'

'Gone, madame. They're all gone. There's just me here. There's a fire in hardware too, in the paint store. I've told the police about that.'

'Good girl. Now ring round all departments and say they must evacuate. The stairs are all right. Tell them that, the stairs are all right. Remind them not to use the lifts. Got that?'

'Yes, madame. That is what I am doing.'

'Have you spoken to the manager?'

'He's gone too, madame. He is already out in the street. I can see him from my window.'

The senior saleswoman used a word she thought she had forgotten.

'Right, Marie. When you have spoken to each floor, get out yourself. Understand?'

'Yes, madame.' The kid was gulping back her fear.

.   .   .   .   .

'So that is how the interest rates work.' The bank manager was smiling benignly. He liked this couple. Luxemburgers were a dour lot usually but this pair looked as though they were going places. German-speaking, of course, but what did that matter with the Common Market. He began to take out leaflets that the bank handed out to prospective customers. There was the sound of sirens, many of them, wailing in the distance. The bank manager felt the hair prickle on the back of his neck at the approaching urgency of the sound. His accountant pushed the door open without knocking.

114

'Monsieur, excuse me, there is a big fire at the store down the road. It is terrible, there are people trapped there, and again at the office block just round the corner. It is catastrophic.'

He was holding the door open with his hand and looked round sharply as a body pushed through behind him, then stared in disbelief at the pistol that a girl was pressing into his side. The manager was half out of his seat as Diamond One leaped round the desk and took him round the neck, hand over his mouth. Sapphire One walked calmly to the door that led from the manager's office to the main counter area. She opened the door a crack. Diamond One released the bank manager as Sapphire Two moved into the room covering him and the accountant. Diamond One opened his brief-case and passed Sapphire One a machine pistol. He nodded and, together, they stepped into the area behind the counters. Diamond Three and Diamond Four had just come in through the main doors. They dropped their bundle of skis and locked the doors, hanging up a 'Closed' notice.

There were two tellers and the manager's secretary behind the counter. They were already on edge from the screaming sirens and they obeyed the pointing machine guns and backed away from their counters without making any attempt to press the alarms. Diamonds Three and Four lifted the flap in the counter and raced up the stairs to the offices above. The two girls and one male clerk were standing on tiptoe, leaning out of the window to watch the blaze. They gasped in horror at the sight of the pistols and the male clerk fainted, his head cracking against a desk as he went down. Diamond Four covered the frightened group while Three went to the switchboard and jerked out the main lead, crushing the plug under his heel. Three shepherded the woman down the stairs while Johann Walther pocketed his gun and grasped the male clerk's wrists, dragging him along the floor and on to the staircase.

The manager had made no protest. Bank instructions were explicit. If there was danger to life the bank had to lose its money. Nevertheless, managers who put up a fight seemed to get promotion; those who didn't, didn't. The manager decided he could do without it. Humbly he acknowledged the keys on the chain round his waist. The accountant looked appealingly at him, then shrugged and produced his own key.

The strong-room was down a flight of steps, closed off by a grill door. Behind that was the strong-room door itself. Inside the strong-room were five million francs, an enormous sum accounted for by the two sub-branches and the wages bills of the seven factories and stores that drew on this branch for funds at the end of each month.

Diamonds Two and Three and Sapphire One produced plastic bags and began to fill them with notes. Anything below one hundred francs they ignored. They worked deftly, stuffing the thick bundles in, bulging out the sacks. They knew already that each sack would hold seven thousand notes, fourteen thousand per person, forty-two thousand between the three of them. Half a million pounds, near enough. When the bags were half full, Sapphire Two and Diamond Four backed out of the strong-room, leaving Diamond One to cover the staff.

The two of them let themselves out of the back door of the bank, leaving the spring locks jammed open. They walked calmly down the alleyway that opened out on to the car park. Cerise Nolan watched them starting up the two cars. The number plates would change automatically five minutes after the getaway. They would transfer to a different car, a chauffeur-driven Mercedes 6000 within ten kilometres. She tensed and gripped the binoculars tightly and felt the sweat break out on her neck.

.   .   .   .   .

Jacques Fruyeaux had been a *gendarme* for fifteen years. He had never made any rank because he had never been able to pass the examinations. He was, however, one of the best men in the district with one of the highest arrest records in crime and an impeccable relationship with the public. He was just about to earn his promotion despite his lack of academic distinction.

He had been to the scene of the fire in the department store and had been back to the station to collect the disaster kit. Unlike most of his colleagues, his whole attention was not distracted by the fires and his policeman's eyes had caught the 'Closed' notice in the glass doorway of the bank. For a second he hesitated, then stepped on the brake. He unclipped the microphone and spoke to operations.

'Fruyeaux here, my angel. I'm stopping to investigate the bank on the corner of . . .' He glanced round and gave the name of the cross streets. The girl's voice squawked back at him.

'The inspector says . . .' Then the inspector himself was on the radio.

'Fruyeaux, get that kit out to them fast. You hear ?'

'OK, Inspector, just one second to make sure.'

He clipped the microphone back into its mounting before there could be a reply. It was probably nothing but his instinct was prickling. Once on the pavement he could see the moving figures inside the bank, saw the huddled group and the menacing shadows behind them. He drew his pistol and turned back to the car and the radio.

Cerise Nolan had the cross-hairs of the telescopic sight dead centre on his chest. For a second she forgot who she truly was and realization came flooding back only just in time. She raised the rifle-tip a millimetre and squeezed the trigger. The silencer allowed only a slight *phut* of escaping gas.

The shock of the bullet smashed Fruyeaux to the pavement. It had angled down, tearing the ligaments of his shoulder and clipping his scapula before it broke the skin at the exit hole in his back. Fruyeaux had been shot before and the second time wasn't half as bad. The pain was bloody awful though.

Now that he was on the pavement he was covered by the car door and he dragged himself, until he could get an elbow over the edge of the floor of the car. He almost fainted with pain as he reached up for the microphone, dragging it out of its clip, pressing it close to his mouth, shouting urgently with pornographic embellishment until he finally slumped unconscious.

Cerise Nolan was also speaking urgently.

'Come in, Topaz Five! Are you there, Topaz Five?' At last the missing Topaz Five answered.

'Blockade action, general alarm. Let the escape cars out, then blockade. Acknowledge.'

'Topaz Three OK! Topaz Four OK! Topaz Five OK!'

By now the bank staff were being locked in the strong-room and there was little left to do when Topaz One came through with the alarm, just a slam of the doors and a twist of the locking lever. Then they were out, sprinting to the cars.

The cars had barely covered a hundred metres before Topaz Three, Four and Five stepped out from their respective positions and threw paper bags of tricorne spikes into the road. Whichever way they fell a point stood sharply upwards and no vehicle could approach or pass the bank without tearing its tyres. At the same time thick clouds of tear-gas smoke began to pour from cylinders that had been dropped on the pavement.

The control room in Geneva picked up the 'All's well' message and Fafner was called in to hear the final reports. The two cars were well away and pursuit had been wholly thwarted. Fafner looked at his secretary and smiled. He turned back to the controller and asked a question. The answer crackled back over the scrambler.

'Yes, the fires were still burning. Only two ambulances had left and there was much loss of life.'

Fafner's smile broadened. Things were going well, once more. The Montague girl must now be killed. A successful escape from the Wolves could not be tolerated. And there was Videl of course. He would have to make an example of him. He chuckled at a sudden thought. Why not let Videl kill the girl first? He called Inge Ludwig and dictated an operational order and a telex before turning back to the control desk. Everything was still as it should be. The fires now seemed to be out of control.

.   .   .   .   .

Marie Daudin had left her switchboard. There was nothing more she could do and she was crawling on her hands and knees along the corridor that led to the back stairs. She was a shrimp of a girl and crawling was not difficult. Only twenty more metres to go and then she could run down to safety.

She felt the explosion before she heard it – a great lung-squeezing constriction that clutched at her throat and stopped her breathing. It was, in fact, the main oil tank that fed the central heating that had gone. It blew out the ceiling of the corridor and slabs of concrete jagged with twisted re-inforcing metal crushed down around her, while the wave of flaming oil followed closely behind.

It was an hour before the firemen got to her and by then she had been dead for fifty minutes.

.　　　.　　　.　　　.　　　.

In London the director read the reports and caught his lower lip between his teeth. It was the only way he could stop the trembling. The bank job in Nice was simply horrendous and Manet's execution had caused every terrorist organization to lick its lips in envy. And now, for the first time, there were hints that the Wolves were loose in England. Nothing admitted yet but the director could sense it, feel the hesitation before people answered. He dialled Scotland Yard on the direct line and asked for Mealie Jimmy. The flat northern voice did nothing to reassure him.

'Yes, we're investigating now. Should know by Tuesday. No, not until Tuesday. No, we can't hurry it, it has to be Tuesday, you ought to know that!'

Mealie Jimmy slammed down the phone and muttered, 'And up yours too, you old sod!' He pressed the bell for Deckham and sniffed as the little fairy came prancing in.

'All set for Tuesday, Deckham?'

'Yes, sir.'

Mealie Jimmy stared and let the contempt deepen in his eyes.

'All right, little man, don't come the old soldier with me. Let's have it. I want the lot – everything!'

Deckham swallowed, his throat jerking spasmodically. He began to go through the preparations that had been made for the Tuesday evening visit to the laboratory in Camden Town. He had picked good men, he could assure the consultant of that! There was just one thing he kept back, fearful of the scorn that would be poured over him.

13

Tuesday was a foul day in Camden Town. The wind blew the fine rain at an angle, penetrating mackintoshes, throwing umbrellas into swooping, twisting confusion. People kept off the streets if they could and if they couldn't they walked quickly, shoulders hunched, heads down, hands in pockets, watching the puddles as they went.

The inspector, authorized under the Factories Act to inspect all industrial premises where manual work was carried on, stood under the shelter of a rusting iron canopy in the yard of the pharmaceutical firm, listening to the production manager's grumbles. He nodded now and again to show he was interested, but his eyes were following the movements of his three assistants, who were unloading the van. It was mostly measuring equipment but there were dust filters and one or two items of boxed equipment with dials. Two of the assistants were in blue denim overalls and they were genuine employees of the Factory Inspectorate, as was the inspector himself. The third assistant wore a black jump suit and was less deft in handling the equipment.

The inspector sighed and grunted.

'Aye, they're a devil these spot checks, but my lads know what they are doing and we won't cause a mess.' He cocked an eye at the production manager. 'You haven't made any changes since the last full inspection, have you?'

The production manager shook his head vigorously.

'Well then, nothing to worry about, have you?' He stamped his feet to get the circulation going. 'Now, sir, if you will let my lads roam about, they'll take their measurements and do their tests and I'll have a general look round myself. That all right?'

The production manager shrugged and mumbled a grudging acquiescence. The factory inspector smiled grimly and jerked his head at the lads.

'Come on, boys. In out of the wet.'

The team moved into the factory and began measuring and testing to ensure that conditions complied with the stringent regulations of the Factories Acts. At four-thirty they had reassembled in the main yard. The inspector watched the two of them loading the van.

'Hello, where's Tom?'

'Tom left early, remember. His missus is expecting like.'

'Oh! yes. That's right. Well, clear off when you're ready, lads.' The inspector turned to the production manager.

'All looks OK, sir. The guard rail round the boiling pans should be four inches higher but we won't prosecute for that. Let us know when you've raised it and we'll come round and have a look.' He smiled and turned away towards his car. He was mentally keeping his fingers crossed for Tom, who should be pretty uncomfortable by now, stuck up in the roof cavity of the laboratory.

.   .   .   .   .   .

Deckham had come on the laboratory job himself. He hadn't told Mealie Jimmy that he was doing it himself and he knew what would happen if there were any slip-ups. He felt the nervousness at the back of his throat. He leaned forward and took a sip of his beer.

The man sitting opposite him had a hearing aid – a flesh-coloured earphone and a lead going down to an amplifier which protruded from the top of his jacket pocket. They were at a corner table in the pub fifty yards down the road from the factory. It was just past five-thirty and there were few people in the place. The man with the hearing aid ducked his head and tried again.

'Can you hear me, Tom? We haven't had anything from you for the last fifteen minutes.'

To anyone observing him he appeared to be speaking to Deckham. Deckham saw his face change and he spoke quickly to cover the faintest of squawking noises that were coming from the earphone. He looked expectantly at the other man, waiting until he glanced up to meet his eyes. The other man nodded.

'The place seems to be clear now. He'll give it another ten minutes then he'll come down and set up the bugs.'

Deckham felt the tension swelling up inside him. If Tom made a mess of things he, Deckham, would be truly in the shit. He reached out for his beer and drank convulsively. The Brass Turnbull lead had taken them nowhere. Brass had gone abroad, they said. Would be away three months. And now if Tom slipped up he'd have nothing to offer.

Tom Backhouse was not likely to make a mess of things. He was a small, precise man, only just over the minimum regulation height for a policeman. This made it difficult to climb down out of a roof space and he had to hang by his hands before dropping lightly to the floor.

The laboratory was some forty feet by twenty. There were half a dozen benches in rows and racks of bottles round the walls. There was a table at the far end of the room and a blackboard behind it. There was sufficient light filtering up from the security lamps in the yard to see to move around but the laboratory was on the second floor and he had to use his torch to inspect the underside of the table. It was this tiny flash of light that was seen by the production manager as he crossed the yard to his car.

The production manager stopped and stood, perfectly still, waiting for the flash of light to be repeated. There was nothing more and after a moment he went back into his office and took up the telephone. When his call was answered he spoke urgently for a moment, then listened to his instructions. As he put the phone down he felt his hands sweating slightly.

Tom Backhouse had almost finished. He was working deftly and quickly, screwing the bugs into position, not relying on tape or pins. As the last screw set firmly home he gave a grunt of satisfaction and began to pack his tools into a canvas roll. He snapped the press studs together and straightened up. He already knew the door to the staircase was locked but there was a fire-door with a panic bar giving on to the fire escape and there would be no trouble about getting out. A window had been left open to air the room before the evening class and he went over to it and cautiously pushed it wide open. He was humming a tune under his breath and he was satisfied with a job well done. He had keys to the wicket gate, keys that had been cut during the lunch-break after one of the lads had taken an impression from the lock. No, there would be no trouble getting out. He only hoped he didn't want a pee while he was back up in the roof. He hummed more loudly as he leaned out of the window. He didn't hear the soft footsteps crossing the room.

The hands round his ankles sent a spasm of fear retching up into his throat. He tried to hold on to the window frame but it was too late. Then he was out, head first and plummeting down, two storeys to the concrete of the yard below.

In the pub the man opposite Deckham sat up sharply and put a hand to his earpiece.

'Bloody hell, Tom must have sneezed. Nearly blew my eardrum out that did. Can't think why we haven't heard from him. I'll call him up.'

He began to mutter, as if in low conversation with his companion. There was a puzzled frown on his face.

'Tom, come in, man! We're worrying about you. Come in, Tom!'

He looked at Deckham.

'Tom's off the air good and proper.' Deckham did not reply but put out his hand and touched the other man lightly on his knee.

'The doors are opening, one leaf of the main door. Stay here, I'm going out to take a look.'

He left the pub, letting in a blast of cold wet air as he went. He walked briskly up the road, watching the car as it drove out of the factory yard. The driver had his coat collar turned up against the rain and Deckham could get little in the way of a description as the man got out and pulled the gates to behind him. Deckham went on up the road and round the block before going back to the pub. He brushed the raindrops off his mac before taking it off. He shook his head at the other man.

'Couldn't see much. Must be a late bird. No cause for alarm. We'll move on to the café in half an hour and wait for the class to arrive. OK?' The other man nodded.

They waited in the café a full hour and a half in the smoke-filled steamy atmosphere before they gave up. Repeated calls to Tom to come in had gone unanswered. Deckham had got beyond the stage of fear. He knew something was badly wrong – the class hadn't turned up and there was nothing from Tom. He knew he was right in it. *Right* in it. He looked at his watch.

'Call up the beat copper. We'd better go in and take a look.'

He had a key to the main gate and he, an accredited detective of the Metropolitan Police, and a uniformed constable would find the gate unlocked and investigate. It took only two minutes for the uniformed man to stroll up to the gate at the regulation two miles an hour.

Deckham was in such a state of nerves he thought for a moment the key wouldn't work. He deliberately relaxed, tried again and the gate swung open. The constable had been specially briefed and he needed no instructions.

'We'll just take a walk round like, shall we, sir?'

Deckham nodded, glad that the initiative had been taken from him. The constable's torch with its broad beam flashed into the corners of the yard, then fastened on a bundle of rags on the concrete under the laboratory block. They walked over to it and stared down at the remains of Tom Backhouse.

Deckham felt the bile rising and knew he would vomit in front of the constable if he stayed.

'Get on to the station!' he gasped, then turned and hurried from the yard. This was *it*. The Brass Turnbull lead had petered out – and now *this*! Mealie Jimmy would have him fried for breakfast for this. An orgasm of fear exploded inside him.

. . . . .

At an hotel in the Cotswolds another orgasm was on its way. Juliette Montague relaxed and enjoyed its coming. Since she had been living with Rigbey she had found her mind switching to thoughts of the happier memories of the past, to inconsequential things, to old forgotten whimsies as he made love to her. Wryly she realized it must be a hang-over from her marriage, when she switched her mind to anything rather than the grisly business in hand. But now the thoughts were happy thoughts.

As Rigbey moved above her she was smiling. Sometimes she felt as if she was flying but tonight it was sailing, watching the bubbling crest of the waves coming closer, feeling the boat rise to meet them and dip sharply as they passed. It was a superb boat and the tiller was of varnished teak.

And now she was back in her childhood, at a country fair. She was in a swing boat, a vague shape in front of her, straining at the rope. She felt herself swinging up and then the jerk, softened by yielding flesh, the tug of effort, then the back swing. She let her head fall sideways and succumbed to the dizziness.

The scene changed. She was in Spain, in Pamplona, and the bulls were running the deep tunnels of the streets. She felt the pounding hooves, saw the flowing muscles as the horned heads turned and quested every opening as they ran. The drumming got louder and the hooves were tearing at the ground, as they burst into the arena.

And then she was soaring. Higher and higher and then higher again. A moment before the explosion she had one final image. A volcano erupting, throwing out white-hot, red-hot, bronze-hot lava in thick waves.

She made sure it was over before she let her muscles soften. She stirred lovingly in his arms. He was still moving inside her, letting her down gently. She purred with contentment.

Rigbey looked down at the satiated smile. If only! If only he could love this girl, who gave herself to him so completely and who demanded nothing from him.

Juliette looked up at him. She ran a finger across his forehead, wiping off the beads of sweat. She felt contentment but fear went with it. She tried to voice her fear.

'Darling, promise me one thing.'

He rubbed his forehead against her cheek.

'Darling, promise me that when you get tired of me you'll let me down easily.' She went on hurriedly, fearful of being misunderstood. 'I don't mean you have to be kind to me and go on when you want to stop. I mean . . .' She hesitated. '. . . well, I mean, can you just give me a hint. I'll take it, I promise I will – I'll keep away from you and just . . . well, just walk away.

But, please, never slap me in the face when you've had enough – just let me know . . . *kindly*, and I'll go – I won't cling, I promise.'

Rigbey felt embarrassment tying his tongue. She must have sensed it, realized that he didn't really care – that she was good in bed and nicer to be with than without but realized that there was nothing deep, nothing more than that. He felt a surge of guilt and smoothed back her hair with his hands. He kissed her lips and said comforting things and knew that he lied when he said them.

She moved away from him and swung her legs off the bed. She was always shy with him afterwards and she looked away as she pulled a gown round her naked body. She went to the bathroom, toes wriggling in the thick pile of the carpet, luxuriating in the opulence of the bedroom.

James Rigbey could hear the splashing from the bathroom as he was dressing. He looked at himself in the mirror and grinned. Rest and recuperation they had called it. For her, not for him. But they had decided she needed him around, if she was to make a proper recovery. They were safe enough – embarrassingly safe. A courting couple followed them wherever they went; they never dined alone and only in their bedroom was there complete privacy. But it was worth it. A suite in the loveliest hotel in the Cotswolds was something even the Americans blanched at paying for and it was all on the firm.

The bathroom door was open. He walked over to it and put his head round. She had heard him coming and was staring at him with smiling eyes, half embarrassed. She was lying on her back and her breasts made two peaked islands. Lower down dark curls floated upright, moving gently in the water. Her mouth had the half-pouting beginning of a kiss and she was blinking her eyes rapidly.

James Rigbey felt the guilt low down, moving upwards into his throat. This girl would crawl over broken glass to get to him and yet he knew he could never give her the love that she needed. He enjoyed her company, she was better in bed than most, but – yes, *but*. There was no feeling of desperate loss when she was not around – no yearning for her, no surge in the bloodstream every time he saw her. He grinned at her, winking.

'I'll dry you, if you hurry.'

She was up in one swift movement, dripping water, and he had the towel ready. He folded it round her, holding her tightly pressed to him. He saw the tears in her eyes.

14

'Deckham, I'm beginning to think that you are just about the most useless object the police have ever been stuck with.'

Mealie Jimmy was enjoying himself. He sat back in his chair, forcing his great bulk against the springs, while Deckham stood white and silent before him. If only the little twit would answer back, show he had something inside him except jelly. He made up his mind to put Deckham on the transfer list. But first kick him a bit more, make him grovel.

'So last night was a complete and utter pig's dinner, was it?'

At last Deckham spoke.

'No, it wasn't. It showed us that there is something wrong in North London. Tom Backhouse would never fall out of a window. And the class didn't turn up and the address of the class instructor is phoney and there's definitely something on and it fits the pattern of the Wolves.' Deckham ran out of breath.

'But what about the staff at the factory, Deckham?'

'It was the production manager who fixed the classes. *He* says he was approached by a seemingly respectable lecturer and saw nothing wrong. Anyway, he's still around so that is some sign that he's straight.'

In this Deckham was wholly wrong. The production manager had left home that morning and driven straight to the airport. He was, at that moment, in the air on his way to Stockholm. When Mealie Jimmy heard about this he would burst at the seams but Deckham had not yet finished.

'There's one other thing. The whisper is out that Brass Turnbull is dead. He was seen being taken in a car by two men and our informant says he looked dead already.'

'So you think the Wolves are here, do you, Deckham?'

'Yes, I do.'

Mealie Jimmy stared at him. There was a knighthood vacant at the moment and one of the Yard's consultants would get it. It was going to be him if he could break the Wolves. Keep his bloody wife's mouth shut for a bit and let him retire finally with complete satisfaction. And they gave him clods like Deckham to work with! Stir the little pansy up a bit more.

'Deckham, when you speak to me you say "Sir".'

Deckham swallowed twice then jerked out the words. 'Oh! No! "Sir" is a sign of respect.'

He closed his eyes, waiting for the storm. There was silence from Mealie Jimmy. Deckham looked at him. What the devil was the old shit laughing at? Surely the Wolves *were* in England.

The Wolves were in England with a vengeance. North London had gone to ground after the security scare but South London was in a fully operational state. The killing of Brass Turnbull had taken them all through the barrier and they no longer had any doubts about their ability. They were now assured of their resolution, confident of success and wholly dedicated to their cause. Preparations for the big job were beginning. There was no planning to do; that had all been done in Geneva but there was a great deal to be done in the way of preparation.

A young man and his girl spent their evenings wandering round the dingy streets at the back of Waterloo station, looking at furnished flatlets and rooms to rent. Four young men, operating separately, examined the car parks in the area, listing times of opening and closing and watching the security arrangements. Another couple spent a great deal of time on the river between Westminster and the Tower of London, riding up and down in the ferries and hiring a rowing boat each evening to make the journey themselves. The boy did a lot of lazing while the girl did most of the rowing. They became a familiar sight to the men who had an interest in watching the river. There was also a secondary operation to be put in train.

A telex had come in late at night. The duty clerk of the South London pack had rolled off his camp bed, cursing. In case the clatter of the telex was not enough to wake the night staff, there was a bleeper on the wall beside the bed. He stabbed irritably at the stop button, strolled over to the telex and smiled maliciously. It began:

'Immediate for Agate One.'

It then lapsed into code in five-letter groups, rattling at the speed of a machine gun as the tape was fed into the machine in the operations room at Geneva.

The clerk let it run and went to the telephone. The leader of the South London pack answered almost at once.

'Hello, Bill, it's the office here. Can you get over right away? There's an "Immediate" coming through on the telex.'

There was no grumbling at the other end, just 'Right I'll be over at once.'

There were twenty lines of telex. The clerk tore the top copy off the machine and laid it out ready on the desk. It was going to be a long job decoding that one.

Bill arrived within fifteen minutes. He was a large man, a solicitor with a lucrative practice. He sat down at the desk and worked quickly and efficiently. He noted the use of the operational code name and at line five he paused and whistled softly to himself and put a query mark against the word then carried on to the end of the message. He laid down his pencil and sat back in his chair and read the message through again before drawing a scribbling pad towards him and drafting a response. He turned to the clerk.

'Could you send this through to Basel, please?'

The clerk looked at it. It read: 'Please confirm last four groups of line five.'

The clerk took the draft to the machine and began to punch out the message in clear. He sat back and waited a moment before the machine chattered back at him. 'Min Pse will revert after checking.'

Ten minutes later the machine came to life again sending out a stream of letters. Agate One leant over the message and began to work at the decoding. It took only five minutes to get it. The second message ran :

'Yes. Words are quote, thereafter execute, repeat execute. Unquote. Method left to you but should be impressive to local staff to ensure maximum loyalty in forthcoming operation.'

Agate One sat back in his chair and drummed with his fingers on the desk top. Stone the crows, South London was going to come to life with a bang. What with their first killing successfully completed and with setting up the big job – the *really* big job and now this. Method left to him! He stared at the ceiling and grinned slowly as the ideas began to form. Yes, that should be impressive enough and all kept in the family too. He got up from the desk, still grinning and leafed through the non-immediate telexes that had come in that evening. Two were about this fellow Videl, but those arrangements were all tied up. The car was waiting, with a driver who knew the Cotswolds and the rifle and the other equipment was all ready. There was only his reception tomorrow morning and now, after this telex, the evening's fun. He grinned again when he thought of Videl.

.　　　.　　　.　　　.　　　.

In Geneva, Streicher passed the South London telex to Fafner, who read the decoded message and nodded. Agate One was right to query the order. It was, after all, a most unusual one. He dropped the telex on his desk and pressed the button that brought Inge Ludwig into the room. He waved his hand towards an armchair and she sat down, ankles demurely crossed, hands in her lap. He showed her the telex and she read it impassively and made no comment. Fafner watched and cleared his throat.

'Inge, my dear, I have almost decided to bring the Nolan girl into our head office to fill the vacancy which Videl will leave. Her record is impeccable and she did brilliantly in Nice. My only doubt, my dear, is how you would like having another woman in the operations team.'

He watched her face carefully as she thought before answering. She waited a long time before she spoke, choosing her words carefully. She was trying to eliminate any emotion from her thinking, any suggestion of a thought that perhaps Fafner wanted the girl for reasons other than her efficiency as an operator. She dismissed the thought. He could have a dozen women if he wanted. But then, of course, they wouldn't be safe, wouldn't be as secure as the Nolan girl would be. She would have to be very careful indeed in what she said.

'I think I would resent her at first but, if she was good and amenable to authority, I would be able to like her. I also have been checking her record and it is indeed excellent.'

Fafner wondered whether he should give the woman some words of reassurance. Mother of his children she might be but she could never be sure, never be truly sure that he would keep her. He decided not to speak. She had answered sensibly and there was no need to remove the slight sense of insecurity he had seen in her face. He smiled.

'Very well, Inge. We will move her up to Geneva for a trial. Three months in the outer office, no access to the operational planning. I would be glad if you would make use of her personally, I would value your opinion of her and you must have her close to you. Now could you get me the latest progress report on the London job.'

Inge Ludwig waited until her back was towards him before she pursed her lips and let the concern show in her eyes.

．　　　．　　　．　　　．　　　．

Videl was in a Cotswold village. He glanced at his watch. Reassured, he turned back to the sniper's rifle that lay disassembled on the bed. The arrangements had been exceptionally good. There had been no problem about the crossing or Customs and the car had been waiting as arranged. He began to screw the silencer on to the barrel. Once the weapon was complete he took practice sightings out of the window, standing well back so that he should not be seen from the street.

Satisfied, he put the gun back on the bed, and went to the window, this time making no pretence of concealment. The weather was fine – the crisp sunshine of early winter – nothing to hold them back from their afternoon walk. Another half-hour and lunch would be over. He went back to the bed and began to strip down the rifle. He knew exactly where he would wait for them.

．　　　．　　　．　　　．　　　．

Rigbey took Juliette by the hand. The lovely Cotswold street glowed with yellow sunshine, belying the coldness of the wind. Juliette was wearing a tweed cape and leather fur-lined boots and Rigbey felt her body softly moving beneath the rough cloth. Their guards, a young dark-haired man and an even younger girl, came out of the door of the hotel a minute later and followed them.

They turned into a side lane and began the gentle climb up a grass-covered path that would bring them out on top of one of the rolling hills, a path that would give them a choice of ways across the countryside. Their shoulders brushed together and their fingers were entwined and the woman's eyes sparkled as she talked to the man who walked beside her. Their way was becoming steeper and soon they would be within sight of the copse, where Videl had chosen his concealment.

Rigbey was talking about paintings and the joys of the Turner exhibition he had seen in Zürich. She answered him lightly, delighting in anything he had to say, asking a question now and then to keep him talking, basking in the sound of his voice.

In the lair he had constructed, Videl brought the rifle up into his shoulder. It was their favourite walk and he knew where they would emerge. They would be only fifty metres away and with a telescopic sight he could hardly miss. The two heads came into view, bobbing and swaying in the unnatural foreshortening of the telescope. Their shoulders were above the brow of the hill as Videl took his eye from the sight to check the range. In that moment Rigbey and the woman turned off from the path that would bring them towards him and were instantly masked by the bushes. Videl cursed and waited for them to emerge but saw only a blurred image through the sparse leaves before the two heads dropped out of sight.

Slowly Videl eased on the safety catch and crawled along the edge of the trees. A rocky outcrop angled down the hillside and he took its shelter, working his way towards the two lovers. He saw the tweed cape first. She had taken it off and it hung over a tree stump. Videl squeezed himself forward another two feet.

Rigbey looked at the face of the woman who loved him. Eyes the colour of smoky quartz gleamed at him. The full mouth was parted slightly and he could feel the warmth of her breath. One hand was on his thigh, kneading the muscle, the other on his shoulder pulling him gently towards her as she tipped her face up for his kiss. He would try to make it seem sincere.

There was no sound, only a terrible sensation of tremendous force, then the smack of lead against bone and flesh and Juliette's body jerking out of his hands — jerking away as though she had been struck with a sledgehammer. For a second he saw her left cheek opened out into a bulging pink meaty cavity with the whiteness of the bones showing through, then the blood surged inwards from the edges covering the wound in a red veil.

He went down on one knee and scooped her into his arms. She was rigid with shock and the ghastly ruin of her face stared up at him despairingly. On the edge of his vision he saw a young girl sprinting up the hillside, mouth open, sucking in air in great panting breaths of anxiety. She slowed, then crouched, both arms out in front, hands clasped together as she began to fire methodically with a long-barrelled automatic pistol. The young man ran past her, revolver drawn but unfired.

Rigbey bound Juliette's face with his handkerchief and scarf, then took her up in his arms again and began to walk slowly back to the village. Her hands drooped towards the ground and the soaking blood splashed in a long trail behind him.

15

Videl got away. The second car was waiting just before the motorway and an hour and a half later he was running into London. The safe house was in Battersea and he approached it cautiously. It was in the middle of a row, three-storeyed with a basement area. The door opened as he climbed the steps and a woman wearing a white tee-shirt and crumpled jeans stood back to let him in. She was a West Indian, with the high cheek-bones and long black hair of a Trinidadian. She was in her early thirties and strong white teeth flashed as she spoke.

'Name rank and number, man?'

Videl looked at her in surprise. She laughed.

'OK. OK. Don't sweat, man! Just give me the words.'

'I like your bijou residence.'

'That's better, man. Now which stone do you like?'

'I'm looking for an agate.'

She moved towards the stairs, beckoning him to follow. She took him to a tatty bedroom.

'You lie up here and we take you off by the river tonight: the lav's down there.'

She pointed down the corridor, then left him, going downstairs to the hallway, where she picked up the phone and dialled. She waited a long time before she had a response. Then she spoke rapidly.

'Yes, he's here. No sign of followers. No, there's no tension, he's very relaxed . . . Right, I know what to do but I don't think it will be necessary. He's not suspicious . . . OK, OK, man.'

She put the phone down slowly and went into the front room to the drinks cabinet with its chipped veneer. She took out a bottle of Mount Gay and poured a two-inch shot. She hesitated before uncapping a bottle of soda and diluting the drink. She took the glass in her left hand and took a deep pull at it while she dug the thumb of the other hand into her shirt, pulling out the elastic of her brassière and running the thumb along, easing it off her body. She was remembering the time when she was a kid at school and the puppies were beginning to eat half their own weight in food every day. Dad had said the time had come and they had taken them out in the car and left them by the side of the road. She remembered laughing at their antics as they realized they were being left behind, scampering and whimpering after the car, tripping and falling over their stupidly large feet. She sighed. As you got older you didn't laugh so much and the scampers and whimpers cut deeper. She swallowed the last of her drink and grimaced with revulsion.

North of the river there was great activity. Two hundred men, inspectors, sergeants and constables, were involved. They were doing the patient questioning that is the backbone of all good police work. There would be the tap on the door, the broad smile from the hatless, or the raised trilby or the three fingers to the edge of the helmet and the soothing opening, 'Nothing to worry about, just routine enquiries,' and then on to the questions.

At nine o'clock that evening Sergeant Tolley had the hunt's first success. It was a lady, who let rooms to young gentlemen. 'Yes, there was Mr John. He went off to those chemistry classes each week and then there was his shooting.' She had seen the gun he'd brought back one evening. 'No, it wasn't a long gun, it was one of those short ones that gangsters used.'

140

From then onwards it was much easier and by midnight the police were beginning to patch together a picture of the North London Wolf pack. Had Geneva known what was happening they would not have been too perturbed. Packs had been discovered before but all routes led back to Basel, not Geneva. There the trail would come to a dead stop. Literally, if necessary.

.   .   .   .   .

South of the river the pack was assembling for the night's fun. The pack was mostly English but not all were Londoners. The broad flat accents of Sheffield rattled along the wharf.

'Eh-up, Sal. Don't forget t'bloody chips, luv.'

They were stacking crates of drinks on the boat while the group was getting its guitars plugged in and testing them with vibrant discord. Rows of coloured lights were switched on and the party began to coalesce, collecting in two and threes.

Videl was on his way to join them. They had fetched him in an old London taxi. The windows had one way vision and they were kept tightly closed. The West Indian girl was with him. Every two or three minutes she would giggle with nervousness. Each time she did it, Videl looked at her suspiciously then turned again to stare straight ahead, hands clasped tightly over his knee.

The party had already started by the time they reached the boat. The West Indian girl and Videl hurried across the concrete and stepped on board. Agate One nodded to the Yorkshireman and the bow and stern ropes were cast off. As they eased into the river the guitars and electric organ started up and the noise burst around them.

'Oi! ducks, 'ave a drink!' The voice was pure cockney – Rotherhithe cockney – and a tattered dolly with turned-up nose and hamster mouth, bee-sting breasts barely outlined by her cable-knit sweater, handed him a ring can of beer. Videl snapped it open and drank.

There were a good twenty people on board. Mostly young; mid-twenties. Videl looked round and noted their resemblance to other Wolf packs he had seen. They looked as though they could handle the big job. He would report favourably when he got back to headquarters.

They were heading downriver and the Tower of London was already past and behind them. The boys and girls were enjoying themselves, dancing hotly to the music, dancing close, holding, fondling, then retreating. They would be down past Greenwich before they started pairing off and slipping out of the fug of the cabin into the cold of the night. The lights of the river banks were fading into the distance as they entered the estuary and the boat began to kick slightly over the short rippling waves that warned of the open sea, not far away.

Agate One worked his way round the edge of the cabin, squeezing past the dancers. He whispered to the group's leader who nodded briefly. The music rose to a crescendo and stopped abruptly. Sweating bodies slowed and came to rest, upraised arms and snapping fingers were lowered as they turned to stare at Videl.

For a moment Videl failed to comprehend his danger. This was England where customs were different. Were they expecting him to speak to them? He was bewildered only for a moment before three young men were on him, tripping him, falling on him, pressing him into the planking. Videl fought furiously until the Yorkshireman stood over the struggling group, dangling a pair of stainless steel chains in his hand. One had bracelets at each end, the other hung free. There was a lank copper sheen to the man's hair – a bastard viking.

'All right, lads. Get t'bugger over on his face.'

The three of them turned him over, forcing back his arms. The Yorkshireman stooped and pressed the bracelets over his wrists.

'Right lads. Let t'bugger up.'

Videl saw the staring faces ringing the cabin. One of the girls was weeping silently, thin tears rolling down pallid cheeks. The West Indian girl had her knuckles up to her mouth, biting and gnawing at them.

They pulled him to his feet, one on either side, one behind him. The faces came crowding round as they pushed him towards the stern, out on to the open deck.

There was a flat slab of concrete lying on the planking, by a section of the rail that had been removed. It had been the counter-weight for an up-and-over garage door. It was two feet by twelve inches and was four inches thick. Two staples were embedded in one end. It weighed forty pounds.

Videl opened his mouth to scream. It was what the Yorkshireman was waiting for. He whipped a rolled napkin over Videl's head, jerked it back between his teeth and tied it behind his head. Videl made anguished noises but they were muffled and would not carry far.

They held his legs while the second chain was looped through the staples of the concrete block then through the eye-holes of more bracelets. A padlock clicked and they stood back. The Yorkshireman looked questioningly at Agate One, who was standing quietly in the background.

Agate One moved forward until he was standing by Videl's side. He turned to the audience and spoke quietly.

'I want you all to watch carefully. All of you must see the penalty of failure.'

He turned and made a brief gesture with his hand. It was Videl's only benediction. Two men took the concrete slab and slid it over the side of the boat. As it dropped the chain tightened and jerked Videl's legs from under him. He fought with his shoulders trying to get a grip on the planking but he slid remorselessly over the side and under the water. As he went the West Indian girl gave a low moan.

Videl had exactly twenty-two more seconds of life while he struggled to hold his breath. Then red lights flashed and his lungs burst apart. His last thought was that they had lied. Drowning *was* painful.

.   .   .   .   .

Videl's dying moments were nothing compared with the agony of the living. Rigbey stepped out into the cold night air from the Intensive Care Unit of University College Hospital. The girl had been brought by helicopter with a surgeon feeding lifeblood back into her almost as fast as it drained away. They weren't sure yet, they said. Couldn't be sure until tomorrow. It was the shock, you see. The wounds were bad enough but the internal bruising was so severe that they wouldn't be able to tell the full extent of the damage until tomorrow. When Rigbey asked if she would be badly disfigured they looked at him first in amazement, then, when they saw the look on his face, with pity, 'Yes,' they had said quietly. 'Yes, there will be disfigurement.'

Rigbey had thought that he was beyond emotion. In his time, when he had been field operational, he had killed three men and one woman. One of the men he had killed with his hands. He had once watched impassively while a man had been tortured. He had been churning sickness inside but he had lived with it and with the memory. Now he felt the aching deep in his body, the wish to cry out, to clench his hands, to bang his head against a wall, to run in circles waving his arms despairingly, to weep, to throw ashes over his head. That it was guilt he recognized, but it made no difference. Through the mists he was arguing with himself. Action! that was what he needed! Action and real danger. Quickly he brushed aside the quick flash of truth – that, really, he wanted death. He looked around him and saw that he had reached Leicester Square. He went down into the Tube station and rode to Green Park. As he walked along Piccadilly he took deep breaths of air. He had to be calm when he got to St James's. They didn't put unstable people on to operations.

16

Rigbey's self-control paid off. The morning's meeting had authorized action and he had been on the midday flight to Basel. Evelyn and the Hardwicke girl were with him. The police had been more than good. They had found a telex message in North London that had escaped the shredder and the number had given them the Basel address. It had not smoothed tempers when the West Germans had said they had known the address for the past year. It was what lay beyond Basel that no one knew. The Wolves had been, as usual, more than clever.

Tassie Hardwicke looked anxiously at Rigbey. He hadn't spoken for the last hour and she feared the look on his face. She had once attended one of the Eastern spy trials and had seen the same look of strained inevitability in the eyes of the accused. He kept fingering something in a bulging jacket pocket.

It was early evening by the time they were ready and no time was to be wasted. The West Germans had saved them a great deal of watching and waiting by providing them with the name, description and address of the link man in Basel. Another hour and it would be dark enough. They had brought little equipment with them. Just the guns the courier had had waiting for them at the airport. They had picked up the car there too – a large Fiat.

Rigbey drove them to the house. It was in a quiet tree-lined road on the outskirts of the city. It was a large house, standing well back with shrubs between the house and the gate.

It was, of course, a professional job. There was the ring of the doorbell and Tassie standing there looking lost, allaying suspicion for just the half-second necessary for Rigbey to swing round the door and get his arm round the man's neck. It was almost over there and then. Rigbey used too much force and they heard the vertebrae crack. He caught himself just in time.

They had found the telex machine and saw how it was done. The incoming machine was connected dir-

146

ectly with an outgoing machine. All messages were punched on tape but they were only passed on if the right coded answers were given. The telex chattered twice while they were examining it but cut off when the right answers were missing.

Now they were in the kitchen with its scrubbed wooden table, Evelyn and the Hardwicke girl standing while their victim sat on a spindle-back wooden chair with Rigbey by his side talking gently to him.

'Name? my friend. Name? Give us your name.'

'Doornfeld.'

'Now, listen, Doornfeld. We must know. *Really* know. Tell us, Doornfeld. Tell us!'

Doornfeld looked at him. This was one of the hard ones. There was no resisting them. He knew his time had come, knew that he had only a few moments more of life. He could prolong it, of course. Tell them everything. But that would mean just a day more to live, then the pack would close in and his death would be slow and painful. They had described it to him – shown him pictures of his predecessor but one. He coughed, agonizingly. He had only three months left anyway. The Wolves used only terminal cancer cases for this job. He was the eighth in line. No, it was time to go. He smiled at them. It was a lined face, grey with illness and the smile was sublime.

'I will tell you all you want to know. There is no need to hurt me.'

He got up slowly and moved towards the hanging cupboard at the back of the kitchen. He had been criminally careless. His capsule was there in its cardboard box. He would have to finesse them. He doubled over, giving his racking cough, letting it all come out, reaching out towards the box.

It was the girl who stopped him. Moving like a snake, she chopped down at his wrist, then took the box, took the pill and broke it open. She looked at the others.

'This one is worth knowing. It's his death pill.'

Things moved quickly after that. They had improvized rapidly. Rigbey had produced the one piece of equipment he had brought with him from London. He had run his fingers over it many times in the plane coming over. It was ten feet of flex with a bayonet plug on one end and a bayonet light socket on the other. They held Doornfeld while they taped the socket over his thumb, wrapping the sticky tape round and round until it formed an obscene bandage, while they plugged the other end in the light. Tassie Hardwicke went to the light switch while Rigbey held the man's face in his hand, fingers pinching the cheeks. He removed his hand and nodded to the girl.

Ten minutes later Doornfeld died. But he died talking.

. . . . .

Across the mountains in Geneva Fafner looked fondly at his secretary. The poor woman was getting over her worries, beginning to smile again. She had a beautiful smile.

'And how are the children, Inge?'

'Well, Herr Fafner, very well.'

'You have no worries about the Nolan girl, Inge?'

The smile that lit up the woman's face brought sunlight into the room.

'I have no more worries, none at all, Herr Fafner. She is too easy with the children but I can correct that, myself.'

'And her work?'

'Excellent. Just as you predicted. Will you excuse me, please, Herr Fafner? The children are ready for their walk.'

She left him and went down in the lift to the doorway to see the children off.

Rigbey tightened his grip on the binoculars and watched the severe tight-lipped woman bend and kiss the two children. She fitted Doornfeld's description. Inge Ludwig – top of the tree. Mistress of the Wolves – or, at least, she was so far as Doornfeld knew. She was the ultimate – the end of the line – the recipient of all the messages.

Rigbey was surprised. That had been a mother's kiss she had given the children and the young girl, with her lithe walk, was obviously the nurse. The Ludwig woman had character all right but was there enough to control an organization like the Wolves? No matter, they would soon find out. They had more equipment now and the going would be easier.

. . . . .

The snowball hit the dark-haired girl full in the face and she shrieked with laughter as she lost her balance and fell into the snow looking up at the boy's gleeful grin. Cerise Nolan was enjoying her new work. The girl pranced round them both, eager for attention.

Cerise looked at the boy's sodden trousers and a guilty qualm brought her scrambling to her feet, brushing snow off her skirt. This would never do. There would be hell from Inge if they went back soaking. And rightly so. Accurately measuring her new mood, the two children fell in by her side and marched across the park with her, each holding a hand. They made a fine picture.

They smiled back at the blonde girl, hair braided round her head, body thickset in its winter clothing, who smiled and beckoned to Cerise. Cerise pushed the two children forward. She was always wary. True, it was a public park but there were few people about and the clumps of bushes gave concealment. Still, it was only a girl and she was on her own and Cerise Nolan was trained to kill men, if necessary. She told the children she would catch them up and turned to the girl as two men appeared, walking calmly towards them. She felt the first fear as the girl stopped smiling and closed on her.

Cerise Nolan fought hard. That it was a girl she was fighting increased her fury. The elbow jab, the knee in the groin – *merde* – not effective against a woman – the ankle kick and all of them countered effectively and efficiently. She had the girl round the neck and postured for a shoulder throw – if only she could get her mouth free and scream to the children to run. Then in a series of blinking pictures like the frames of an ancient movie she saw the two men talking to the kids, saw the smiles and the ready response of the children and she knew it was no longer any good. Suddenly she slumped and let her weight hang on to her antagonist. She heard the low whistle, then the words – English – English in Switzerland.

'Over here, Mark . . . It's all right, she's shamming. But look – she's a professional. She knows all the counters. I had a hell of a time with her. Ask James if she's worth taking.'

After that there had been the prick of a needle and blackness.

When she woke there had been the swollen tongue and grey haze of post-anaesthetic nausea. She looked round the room. There were whitewashed brick walls and a concrete floor. She was lying on a tubular frame bed, covered by grey blankets. A woman in nurse's uniform looked up from the book she was reading and watched her carefully. It was a strange uniform, slightly archaic, a white dress with a purple cape and epaulettes with two gilt pyramidical stars on each. She recognized them as British Army rank markings.

Without speaking the nurse closed her book, got up and went out of the room.

Cerise recognized the man who came in two minutes later. He was one of those who had taken the children. She was beginning to come round but her voice sounded thick and she slurred the English words.

'Are you British Security?'

'Yes.' The man was watching her and she could see the surprise.

'Prove it to me.'

'Why?'

'Prove it to me. You'll see why then.'

'How will we prove it?'

'Let me speak to your contact in Paris – your contact with the French side.'

In ten minutes she was talking to Glasiére on the phone and half an hour later there was a full-blown meeting in St James's Street and she was being called Miss Nolan.

Glasiére was furious and the director had crawled.

'But my dear fellow. How were we to know you had another one on the way up?' The director had spread a hand out in supplication and then had gone on, fawning into the phone.

'Glasiére, there is something big coming off in England, almost certainly in London. We *must* know about it, we really *must*.'

Glasiére had asked to be put back on to the girl – when she picked up the phone they all heard his words.

'Tell them nothing. You hear? *Nothing!*'

After that the atmosphere had been icy and she had been returned to the whitewashed room.

She lay on the iron frame bed, perfectly relaxed. They would have to let her go. She was one of them – or, at least, on their side. It would just be a matter of time.

The door opened so silently that the man was in the room before she realized she was not alone. It was the man they called Rigbey. There was the Hardwicke girl behind him, looking scared. Rigbey was dangling a coil of flex in his hands with a plug and socket on the ends. He pulled up the nurse's chair and sat by her bed. From his pocket he took a brown manilla envelope and shook out a photograph. It was in colour and she felt the nausea rising as she looked at the devastation of the woman's face, the gaping wound, the eyes turned up. The man was speaking quietly.

'You see, Cerise, this was the girl I was going to marry. She meant a lot to me. So you do see, don't you, why you have to tell us . . .'

The Hardwicke girl was shaking him by the shoulder.

'James, you can't, you really can't. She's one of us!'

Rigbey stood up and began to unwind the flex. Shaking her head, Tassie Hardwicke set up the tape recorder. A moment later she was recording the torrent of words.

17

Wolfgang Fafner clutched at the bloody furrows raked down his cheek and jerked his head away in agony. The carefully collected mouthful of spittle spattered full in his face as the woman's contorted mouth shrieked insults. He stepped forward and slapped her hard, then sprang back, stumbling, as she was on him, arms outstretched, nails clawed to tear and rend him. Inge Ludwig had passed the bounds of reason. Her children had been taken and she would kill anyone who stood between her and them, even their father.

Fafner was shocked. It had been more than twenty years since anyone had attacked him physically. His reflexes were wrong and he was humiliated. He backed away from the woman, eager to placate her. Her fury was beginning to descend from the vituperative to the practical.

'You – *you*! Herr Fafner, will go and get them back. Do you think you can trust those oafs. Look at Streicher – the best man you had – losing that girl. What did Videl achieve? – Nothing!' Her voice rose to a crescendo. '*You* will go. *You* will bring back our children. Do you think the man Rigbey will fear to harm them? Did you not hear what happened to Vosper and the Italian? Have you not seen the pictures of Doornfeld's end? He will *kill* them if he has to.' Her voice dropped and she went into the crouch of the tigress ready to spring. 'And if he does, Herr Fafner, you are a dead man yourself!'

Fafner reached out his hands to take her shoulders gently, imploring.

'My dear, calm yourself. You are right. I will go and

you shall come with me. But do not be so afraid. What good will come of taking the children – they are not asking for money. There is no purpose in it.'

She looked at him suspiciously, head on one side, fearing a trap.

'No, there is no purpose that we can see but they are not fools. They got the girl back and beat our men into the ground. They are hard men, Wolfgang – hard.' Her fury subsided now that her objective had been conceded. She smiled thinly.

'I will telephone Elgar. It is time he earned his dividends.'

.   .   .   .   .

Now that they knew what they were up against, or nearly knew, the director had thankfully turned the matter over to Jones and the police. It was operations' concern now, the policy decisions had been taken.

Jones faced Mike Lancing and Mealie Jimmy across his desk. Mike Lancing looked more like a particularly easy-going bank manager than the head of Special Branch.

Mealie Jimmy treated the meeting as if he were in command.

'Right, Jones, let's have it. It's a river job then.'

Jones refused to let his distaste show. Before he had come to St James's Street he had been a colonel of Light Infantry and had subsequently worn the red hat-band and carried the extra pip for a year before discarding his uniform. Blimps had always amused him and he refused to be one. No, it was better to laugh at the shits not to let them score. He answered Jimmy's question.

'Yes, it's a river job. The Nolan girl doesn't know

154

where but it will take a great number of lives. There's someone behind the Ludwig woman. She hasn't seen him but she suspects he's the father of Ludwig's children. Rigbey intended to draw the woman over here by taking the children but it looks as though we may do better than that. Get the father as well. We will pile on the agony, of course. Anyway, it's the Belgians who are going to do the job. That much she did know.'

Mealie Jimmy curled his lip. 'So all we have to do is watch everything between Greenwich and Teddington. That includes the Houses of Parliament, Tower of London, County Hall, the National Theatre, the Festival place and bloody Shell-Mex House. So what are you going to do, Jones?'

'There will be two thousand police in plain clothes north and south of the river between . . .' he bowed slightly '. . . the Tower of London and Battersea Bridge. Any Belgian trying to get into the country will be treble-checked. We have a description of the Ludwig woman and we should get her, at least.'

'Sounds pretty thin to me.' Mealie Jimmy was good at sneering and Mike Lancing almost lost his cool.

'What about this man Rigbey? Sounds a good one.'

'I'm afraid he won't survive this operation. Excessively interrogating an agent of a friendly state is just not allowed. Even though it did give us our only lead. Still, he won't starve. His trust fund owns a thousand acres of outer Coventry and a vineyard in the Champagne country. That's probably what made him so good – not having to rely on his career.'

Mealie Jimmy snorted with laughter, shaking all his three bellies with his mirth. Soft, that's what these buggers were – soft! Bloody poncy private-income sods.

.   .   .   .   .

Wolfgang Fafner and Inge Ludwig entered Britain by the unlikely route of the rail ferry from Larne to Stranraer. No one looked for them and they travelled to London by train and thence by taxi to the outskirts of Woking where Elgar had his mansion.

The house was in the best stockbroker tradition. Built in the 1930s it was set well back in its two acres of wooded garden with a gravelled drive and high stone wall. A middle-aged housekeeper opened the door to them. She smiled bleakly and showed them into a long drawing room that fronted on to a rose garden, dripping now with its winter chill.

Elgar's lean elegance showed in the chalk-striped suit that came from Pooles and the manicured hand he held out to Inge. He offered them sherry, a drink wholly unknown to Inge and one that was distasteful to Fafner. He was feeling uneasy, in alien surroundings, far from his operations room. He glanced nervously at Inge who sat, fully composed, hands clasped in her lap, occasionally reaching out for her glass and taking a sip of the curious brown fluid.

The door opened and Agate One stepped into the room. His full swarthy face showed his curiosity. He had the air of professional competence of a good solicitor and his size gave him presence. Fafner relaxed. He was back in the right atmosphere now.

The conference was crisp and to the point. There had to be a counter-snatch. They would take Rigbey and he would tell them where the children were. They would get them back then. Oh! Yes! They would get them back then. They would get the Birmingham pack on the job. Inge's eyes gleamed at the thought of questioning Rigbey.

·   ·   ·   ·

'Snap!' The girl shrieked the word in an ecstasy of triumph as she slapped down the card. Sarah shrugged despondently. The kid was just too fast for her. She glanced at the boy, happily piling bricks together on the rug before the fire in Sarah's house in Islington. The Fafner children were enjoying their trip to England.

Sarah thought of her barrister and wondered if she oughtn't to have a kid – she could afford to take a year off work and it would be fun. She remembered the well-concealed disappointment of her parents that she had been an only child – poor little bastard though – then she thought of her father the archdeacon and his easy-going but wholly unshakable decency and shook her head in self-reproof. No, she wasn't ready to marry yet, and, yet . . . they would have loved a grandchild. She began to shuffle the cards. It would soon be time for them to go to bed. Just one more round to see if her luck would improve.

.   .   .   .   .   .

Two thousand policemen were having no luck at all. On average each couple had knocked on forty doors apiece and that meant forty thousand households. But the laws of average weren't working for them, and they had turned up exactly nothing.

Detective Constables Nash and Leadbetter were getting bored. They tried their forty-first house. It was one of a long row of peeling villas in Battersea. Nash went up the steps while Leadbetter stayed on the pavement – no need to scare the old dears.

It was a West Indian girl who answered the door. Pretty, high cheek-bones, long straightened hair, about thirty, unmarried. Nash coughed politely and smiled.

She was better than most of them they had interviewed. He used the gambit they had been told to use.

'Excuse me, miss, but we are interested in jewels.'

It was a simple statement that could cover a multitude of follow-ups. Both he and Leadbetter saw the reaction – the sharp intake of breath, the knuckles going up to the mouth, the eyes widening and the stammer as she responded.

'Er? . . . What jewels are you interested in?'

'Well, miss, almost any you might care to name but we're from Topaz One. If that means anything to you.'

Leadbetter moved up the steps and they both saw the look of fear in her eyes. Leadbetter was going to make a supreme policeman in a few years' time. He improvised immediately.

'Could we come in, miss – we need a safe place.'

Her expression softened. This was more like it. Some of the tensions eased and her shoulders dropped a centimetre.

'Oh! . . . I see . . . Come in, won't you?'

She was still uncertain but now it was because of her own inadequacy. She was at a loss. She gestured nervously towards the stairs.

'Up there. You can have the room at the top of the landing. That's where they usually stay. Just shout when you need food.'

Leadbetter nodded and started up the stairs. He patted her shoulder as he squeezed past. Nash followed him, willing to accept his lead.

The room was tatty: an old wooden bedstead and stained mattress, carpet so bare it looked grey, net curtains at the window. Leadbetter closed the door behind him and motioned to Nash to start searching. Nash knew what to do and could go through a room that size in ten minutes. Leadbetter eased off his shoes and opened the door. He could hear the girl moving about below him. Now she was going to the telephone in the hallway. Leadbetter ran swiftly down the stairs, keeping to the inside of the treads. At the last corner he stopped. The girl had her back to him and he could see her dialling. He noted the numbers, then stepped forward closing his hand over her wrist before she could speak. Nash came clattering down the stairs and held her while Leadbetter telephoned the Yard.

Mike Lancing took the message and lost some of his air of placid unconcern. He reached forward and lifted the second phone.

'Get us the GPO – Central – we want a trace on a number.'

In five minutes they had it. Agate One's name was reasonably well known in legal circles and Lancing had a potted history in his hands within half an hour. Ten minutes later the Special Operations room was concentrating on Fulham, where the solicitor had his office. As Agate One drove his car into the vacant lot by the old house, converted into offices, a dozen pairs of eyes watched him as binoculars were adjusted to take in the new range.

Mealie Jimmy heard the news as he was having a snack. He dropped the bones of the fried chicken into their greasy cardboard box and wiped his lips and fingers on the paper napkin. He belched gently, then pressed the bell. He stared up at Deckham.

'Deckham, my friend. First draw a gun, then get a car from the pool. We're standing by, Deckham. We're standing by!'

The knighthood was there – just hovering in the background – and all he had to do was to reach out and grasp it. He lay back in his chair and wondered if he was stupid not to take a gun himself but dismissed the thought. If it came to a shoot-out people looked sideways at a copper who shot the opposition. Not British that wasn't. There'd be no knighthood for a man who used a gun. Oh no! Just walk up to them and do it alone. 'Unarmed policeman tackles armed criminal' that's what the public liked.

.   .   .   .   .

The Belgians were arriving. Three men and a girl. They travelled separately and, as they had French passports, they escaped the special scrutiny that all people from Belgium were receiving. They were the Zircons. Zircons One, Two, Three and Four. Zircon Two was the girl.

There was a cold east wind sleeting fine rain into their faces as they moved towards the base headquarters. Selecting the base had been easy, a house in Wandsworth, but a forward operational base had proved one of the worst difficulties the South London pack had had to overcome. It had to be in sight of the bridge, but, what with the development of Shell Centre, and the old-established institutions round the north side, there wasn't much to choose from. They had tried the area round Waterloo first, but, finally, they had decided the only thing to do was to work from a boat. They had a cabin cruiser moored downstream, which would move up and control the action group while the river-fronting house in Wandsworth would allow them to store their equipment ready for use.

Hungerford Bridge is an anachronism. It should have been torn down years ago but the railways are not in favour of enormously heavy capital expenditure these days. It's safe enough, of course, but it's a hopelessly old-fashioned bridge taking the trains from south of the river over the arches into Charing Cross station. No cars travel on it but many pedestrians use the narrow walkway that will just take two fat people moving abreast. If you don't like heights you avoid it but many commuters on their way to Waterloo take the short cut from the swarming Strand and the teeming environs of Trafalgar Square. It is not a show-piece but it is one of London's most central bridges and when a couple of trains are halted on it waiting to pull in to the station, it probably holds more people at any one time than any other London bridge. It is also the only bridge that could be satisfactorily destroyed by a relatively small quantity of explosive.

The Wolves had assembled a great deal of explosive and they calculated that if they could get it all in position they would have twice the amount they really needed. They had time for the final briefing, for the dress rehearsal, then action the morning after. That was the way of the Wolves – a quick in and out with the overtly criminal acts all done by foreigners, who would be out of the country an hour after the excitement started.

At 7.45 a.m. the next morning as the trains pulled in, packed with the early starters, they hoped to have at least a thousand dead. The greatest train disaster the world had ever known. That would bring the recruits flocking in.

. . . . . .

Agate One liked working under pressure. The bridge job was big enough but to have a kidnapping to organize at a day and a half's notice as well was asking a lot.

They would bring Rigbey first to his office in Fulham. There he would be questioned by Inge Ludwig. What was left of him would be taken to a small coasting steamer, which would put to sea and stay at sea while the rescue of the children and, if necessary, the negotiations went on.

Agate One smiled at the Brummagen man sitting at the other side of his desk.

'Well, that's that then. Your people all know London and you can work on your own but my lot will be backing you all the way. There's the phone and the telex is manned – there's beer in the fridge.'

He got up and left the man to it. He went down the stairs of the old three-storeyed corner house and out into the parking area. His appearance cured a lot of the boredom that had begun to creep in around the immediate vicinity of the car park. The police operations room got three simultaneous calls saying that Agate One had appeared and was about to drive away.

.   .   .   .   .

It was ten o'clock at night and the Belgians were making a reconnaissance of the bridge. Zircon One and the girl Zircon Two, this was to be their only dress rehearsal. Zircon One had the round face of a clown, black tufted sideburns adding a touch of incongruity to the imbecile face. The girl was hollow-cheeked and quivered with intensity. She had been selected because she had killed before – way back in the early days.

Zircon One untied the rope from the ring and pushed off the boat, rowing with short jerky strokes until the current of the ebb tide caught them and pulled them on, down the river. It took them fifteen minutes to reach the bridge and Zircon Two stretched out to catch a stanchion with the grapnel hook. It was just as they had described it and he noted where the carefully measured and shaped containers of explosive would fit and stay in place for the little time that would be necessary.

There was a hiss of oars and a boat entered the next arch of the bridge. A metallic clink showed the grapnel had been secured. That would be Zircon Three and Zircon Four. Zircon One looked at his watch. The escape boat ought to be in position now. He peered into the darkness, became anxious for a moment, then relaxed as the lights appeared, moving upstream in the centre of the channel.

18

The wind howled down the tunnel of the street, rattling windows and causing street lamps to flicker as barren branches jerked and twisted, straining from tree-trunks, whipping and flicking, throwing their shadows on the glistening pavements.

James Rigbey kept his head down and took the force of the wet blast, hands in his pockets, chin tucked in. In the hospital they had been operating until midnight and she was still alive and was going to live; live some sort of a life, anyway. They were sorry, they said, but they just couldn't replace what was no longer there. In layman's language, the cheek-bone had been smashed and the upward pressure had damaged the left eye. The eye would never be fully effective and . . . well, they had gone on for quite a time until Rigbey had left, sickened by the technicalities and the euphemistic jargon.

He came out into Tottenham Court Road and the wide street relieved the pressure of the wind. His breath came easier now and his fingers unclenched in his pockets. He wanted to walk, to think, to go over and over again the agony of guilt, to imagine the love he could have given to this woman, to probe and worry at the remorse that ate into him.

He was aware of the shadows that flickered and rippled around him, the incautious footstep, the hurried whisper, the sharp sideways glance from a passing couple. Tonight or tomorrow, it would happen – probably sooner rather than later. They would take him and there would be pain; the pain of expiation and then perhaps his soul would rest.

He turned westward into one of the side streets, then turned again into Charlotte Street, walking south. The street broadened out to twice its width, vast glistening silence, filling and emptying with the force of the wind. There they took him.

He heard the taxi first, the churning of the engine and the grating gear change, then the shaking note of the diesel as it turned into the street. It was almost abreast of him when there was the quick, urgent patter of feet and they were on him, hands and arms clutching and restraining, pulling, slipping, then grabbing again as he fought them.

In the taxi two of them held him down while a third searched him for weapons. There was nothing to cause alarm. Ballpoint pen, wallet, car keys, a pocket calculator in a leather protective case which opened like a miniature notebook and which advertised a famous building firm. The Brummagen tool-maker, who searched him, pocketed the lot. Rigbey wasn't going to need those things where he was going.

The taxi swung south-west, heading towards Fulham, while on the top floor of the building just off St James's Square a Security Section technician reached out to take up the internal telephone, keeping her eyes fixed on the tiny bleeping point of light that moved almost imperceptibly across the map superimposed on a plastic screen in front of her.

Captain Jones took the call in his office, listened, then walked quickly to the lift. On the top floor he passed through the main communications room with its dozen desks and consoles into one of the special operations cubicles. There were two girls in the room, both plump, both watching their screens intently. The older of the two looked up for a brief moment, reached out a hand and swung the vacant controller's chair round on its pivot.

'He's been taken, Captain Jones. They're moving south-west. I've alerted the watchers round the Fulham house and I've got Car Two moving in from Park Lane to intercept, then watch and follow. Car Four is moving eastwards from Hammersmith.'

Jones nodded and stared at the crawling light. It looked like Fulham. He slid into the controller's chair and reached for the microphone. He called up the specialist army team that had come from Chatham and had been waiting in Hyde Park Barracks for the past four hours. Having set them on their way, he called for Mark Evelyn and Tassie Hardwicke to get them armed and in motion.

In the taxi Rigbey had stopped fighting. There was no need now. The pocket calculator in the Brummagen man's inner pocket continued to send out the signals that were being received in the security operations room and would soon be picked up by Car Two as it came up behind. Later he would be in contact with the top, the very top. He closed his eyes in anticipation, as if waiting for a blow.

.   .   .   .   .

In Elgar's house near Woking, Fafner sat up in the great four-poster bed and listened eagerly to the telephone. Inge Ludwig lay and watched his face. Her lips had gone dry and she clenched her hands under the sheets. He repeated the words for her benefit.

'You have Rigbey and he is at the house in Fulham. Fine! Do not harm him. Be very careful not to harm him at all.' He turned to the woman.

'He is all yours, my dear. All yours!'

The woman had been holding her breath. Now she let it out slowly. Her lips had begun to moisten.

In the car moving towards Fulham she turned towards Fafner and put a hand on his arm, turning to look at him cautiously. She kept her voice low, so that the driver should not hear.

'Herr Fafner. Would you mind if I went alone . . . ?' She paused, almost diffident in her searching for the right words. '. . . I want . . . I want to be wholly uninhibited when I meet with the man Rigbey.'

Fafner looked at her curiously. He knew she had an iron character but the look of anticipation on her face sent ice coursing through his blood. He smiled, but it was an effort.

'Most certainly, my dear.' He looked at his watch. 'The night has gone anyway – three o'clock in the morning. We will be at the headquarters by four and I will leave you there, my dear. I will go to the forward command post and watch the bridge go up from the boat.'

They sat in silence until they reached the house in Fulham. As Inge Ludwig got out of the car, Fafner hesitated, then said, 'Enjoy yourself, my dear,' before the car pulled away, catching out the police who were watching the place and who weren't expecting anyone to leave at that hour. By the time they had the calls out, Fafner's car was lost in the back streets. The air in the Special Operations room was blue as Jones and the two women operators cursed in mutual frustration.

.   .   .   .   .

The light from the street lamps left pools of shadow on the roof of the house opposite the Wolves Fulham headquarters. Tassie Hardwicke, Mark Evelyn and the sergeant of Royal Marines groped their way carefully along the narrow walkway with its twelve-inch protecting wall. The sergeant was carrying most of the equipment and he set it down in the only open space, about a yard square, by a grimy roof window. Downstairs, the owner of the house and his wife were sitting in their dressing gowns, nervously drinking tea and listening to the soothing assurances of the police inspector.

Mark Evelyn heard the bleep of his transistor and held it to his ear, listening for a moment before acknowledging and whispering to the others.

'A woman has just arrived at the house. The car has driven off with two men in it. The police have lost them.'

Tassie nodded, then turned to the Marine, who was fumbling in the darkness with a short metal tube and a tripod. Evelyn and the Hardwicke girl watched him as he grunted with satisfaction and began to feed the shaft of a grapnel iron into the tube. He looked at Evelyn.

'OK to go now, sir?'

Evelyn nodded and there was the soft 'whoof' of low-powered explosive and the grapnel sailed high in a long curve towards the roof of the Wolves head-quarters. It bounced once on the sloping slates' grey surface with an appalling noise, clacking and shrieking as the points dragged across then slithered down, catching for a moment on the parapet before slipping and dropping to the street. Rapidly the sergeant wound in the nylon line, wrapping it round elbow and hand, coiling it for the next attempt. In the street below uniformed police moved out to stop a late-night couple. 'Sorry, sir, bomb alert down here. Would you mind going back? First left, then left again. That's it, sir. Good night.'

The next try was successful. The grapnel caught on the parapet and held. The sergeant pulled hard on the rope, stretching it as taut as it would go, then scrambled round a chimney stack straining to get it yet tighter. He looked at the other two.

'I'd better go first, sir. You can never tell with these old houses. The parapet might be a bit crumbly like.'

Evelyn shook her head.

'No. Tassie goes first. She's the lightest. Ready, Tassie?'

The girl nodded, pulled on her leather-palmed gloves, took a deep breath and went over the side of the house, swinging hand over hand along the rope, legs swaying from side to side, to give her momentum. The rope strained and creaked under the girl's weight and Evelyn gave a sigh of relief as she made a convulsive effort and caught the parapet with one hand, then the other and swung up and over on to the roof.

She lay for a moment panting, letting the strength flow back into her arms and numbed fingers. As she was about to get to her feet, she heard the creak and groan of warped wood as the window of a roof-light began to open.

She moved like a snake, rippling along the edge of the roof on elbows and toes towards the only cover, a chimney-stack four yards away. She got into cover as first a head, then a man's body appeared. Tassie heard him grunt with effort as he squeezed through the window on to the roof. She saw him start and lean over the grapnel hook, blocking her view. She had a long-barrelled pistol with silencer in her hand but a shot now would put him over the side of the house, down past the windows and then Rigbey would die quickly. Suddenly she froze as the man stood up and tossed the loose end of the rope over the side of the house, leaving the grapnel in position. So *that* was what he had been doing.

He began to move towards her, leaning inwards, supporting himself on the sloping tiles of the roof with one hand. It was his worst mistake. Now she could do it. She took careful aim and fired twice, soft plop, plops smashing the man back against the roof, where he slid down into a crumpled heap.

She crawled to him. He was still breathing but the gaping exit holes in his back told their story. She unzipped a thigh pocket of her battle suit and took out her transistor.

'Mark – they heard the noise on the roof. I've killed their man but the rope's gone. Give me five minutes. Exactly five minutes, you hear – then come in from the street. OK?'

'OK, Tassie. We'll be there, don't worry.'

Evelyn and the Marine sergeant scrambled along the edge of their roof, making for the window into the loft. Tassie saw them go – two soft blurs of movement. Five minutes left to save Rigbey from death which would come the moment the front door was forced.

It had to be fast now. Fast and hard. Give them no time to think. Shoot first; they were all enemies, only Rigbey to save from harm. As she wriggled through the roof window, there was a ripple of movement in the streets down below as the heavies got ready to move in.

Tassie dropped through the window into an attic. It was half full of packing cases and she had to pick her way with her torch. Through the door there was a narrow landing, then uncarpeted stairs leading down to the first floor. She went down the stairs two at a time, her rubber-soled boots making soft clumping sounds. She flung open a door and a man looked up, startled, from a telex machine. Shoot first! Don't give them time to think. He screamed as the bullet took him full in the chest. She cursed at missing the head shot that would have kept him quiet. Go on – now – they would be alert in another two seconds.

The second door was the right one. The surprise was still on their faces and they were all three of them still in the positions of arrested movement that the screams had frozen into immobility. Rigbey was strapped to a wooden chair at the side of an old kitchen table. He was bare to the waist and his left arm was fastened to the table by three leather hoops that passed over his wrist, forearm and elbow and which were nailed to the wooden table top. He was only half conscious and the acrid smell of sulphuric acid choked at Tassie's throat. There were two men, one on either side of Rigbey. The woman was at the other side of the table, glass bottle in one hand and the rubber bulb of the dropper in the other. She was dressed plainly in jumper and skirt and there was a single rope of pearls round her neck. Her lips were glistening.

It was all action now. Tassie brought her left hand smashing down over the right, steadying her pistol as she fired. One, two – the first man was going down but the second had his gun almost out of his shoulder holster . . . And one more! The second man clutched at his belly, opening his mouth to scream.

Tassie felt the urgency of the other woman's movements, heard the breath expelled in effort and she flung herself down, rolling, instinctively turning her face into the crook of her arm. The bottle of acid struck the wall behind her and smashed, sending a cloud of fumes into the room.

Inge Ludwig stood and watched the girl climb slowly to her feet. She was a blonde with hair braided round her head. Wide blue eyes stared back at her and flickered for a moment to the remains of Rigbey's arm, strapped to the table.

Inge Ludwig watched her raise the pistol. She stared at the round mouth of the barrel. She had to say something; something to explain, she couldn't die without explaining. She mouthed the words, barely sounding them.

'He took my children. You see, he took my children.'
She saw the pistol jerk and a blow of impossible

force struck her in the middle of the forehead. Her eyes were blinded even before the orange flame erupted from the barrel. And then nothing.

19

Tassie Hardwicke wept for the first time in ten years. She grasped James Rigbey's good hand imploringly.

'James . . . please . . . Please tell us. You've done enough. We can handle it now. Just tell us where and when.'

She shook his arm gently but he stared straight ahead sitting with her in the back of the car that Mark Evelyn was driving through the pre-dawn darkness towards the river. She tried again.

'James, we want to destroy them. We can do it better than you can. Just *tell* us!' Her voice was pleading.

Rigbey spoke in an unnatural monotone. He glanced at her only once. It was an impersonal look.

'No . . . It must be me . . . only me.'

'But, James, let us come with you. James, you might make a slip and then it would be wasted.'

Slowly he shook his head.

'No. Just the boat and two men. No followers. If I'm followed there will be nothing.'

Despairingly the girl let go of his arm as Evelyn swung the car into Chiswick, where the boat would be waiting for them. Just two river patrolmen and a police boat – nothing else. That's how Rigbey said it must be.

She helped him out of the car, holding the door back

to guard his splinted and bandaged left arm. Two hours, the doctors had said. He could go for about two hours more then he would flake out – just fade out into blackness. They would have a hell of a job after that, they said.

Rigbey did not look back as he went down the stone steps to the boat. He stepped on board and the patrolmen cast off.

.   .   .   .   .   .

Mealie Jimmy and Deckham were no longer standing by; they were in action. Deckham was driving one of the unmarked police cars, distinctive only for its larger than usual radio aerial. He was following the fat consultant's directions, patrolling from Southwark Cathedral up to Putney, then over the river and back again on the north side. The reports of the successful raid on the Wolves headquarters at Fulham had brought them both from the standby room in Victoria. It was their second circuit and Deckham found the courage to speak.

'Why are we doing this?'

Mealie Jimmy flashed him just one look of contempt.

'Because, lad, there's going to be all hell out here in an hour or so and you and I are going to be right there with it. Now get on with the bloody driving and keep your eyes closed when the fun starts if you can't stand the sight of blood.'

He sat back in his seat and blessed that bugger Rigbey. If he'd done what he should have done it would be all over by now but the bugger had gone queer and clammed up on them and when you're going to give someone the sack it's no time to be asking favours of him. So that still left the big job wide open.

173

And he was going to be in at the bloody finish. Too right he was. He picked up the hand microphone and called Operations. 'No, nothing happening yet, the only call in at the moment is one from a panda car that is investigating a suspicious movement up towards Wandsworth.' It was one of the sixty calls that had come in over the past two hours. Mealie Jimmy and Deckham had followed up three of them and all had been abortive or petty. crimes. Mealie Jimmy put the microphone down on the seat between them. 'OK, lad, nothing better to do, let's follow this one. We're near enough.' Deckham drove to his directions.

The two constables in the panda car had been fortunate. The Belgians were very good and the site had been well chosen and it was the merest chance that the police driver had seen the shadowy figure humping the bundle down to the riverside. The constable called in on his radio and they made a U turn and went back to have a look.

It was the girl, Zircon Two, who spotted them from the upstairs front window, where she was on watch. She waited a moment to make sure then called up Zircon One.

The driver of the panda car opened the front gate and walked up to the massive bulk of the house, while his companion took the side path that led round to the river. His companion died first. There were two white stabs of flame, two spats of lead and the policeman was down, clutching at himself in the shock of death. The driver turned and ran back towards the car and its radio. Zircon Two took careful aim and knocked him over like a rabbit. At this point, Deckham and Mealie Jimmy were only a few streets away and closing fast.

'There's the car, lad, slowly now!'

Deckham pulled up behind the panda car and the two of them got out. Mealie Jimmy held out a hand, flat palmed. There was a pause while the pig's eyes peered over the rolls of fat, questing, probing the dim light.

'Slowly, lad. This doesn't look right.' Then . . . 'Got your gun, lad?'

Deckham couldn't see what the fuss was about but, then, he hadn't had forty years' experience, didn't have the extra sense that told when danger was real or imaginary, couldn't see the tiny telltale signs that showed a real copper that all wasn't well.

'Right, lad – get out to the left and cover the back, while I radio in. If anything happens, shoot and then get back fast to me.'

'Can't we go together?'

'No, we can't, you windy little bugger. We'll do our pinches the right way. Now get on with you!'

Deckham moved out to the left, picking his way among ornamental shrubs. He made a good target against the light from the street-lamps behind him.

Zircon Two had moved down by the river's edge, lying behind the wall, covering the final loading of the boats. One of them had left, slipping away downriver and the second was almost ready. The charges had been set in the house and the place would be a mass of flames in another five minutes. She sighted carefully and fired low – too low. The bullet took Deckham in the kneecap, sending him screaming to the ground, his revolver flying out into the darkness. Zircon Two cursed. There must be no witnesses left alive. She went forward at a crouching run. She had seen only one man and it sounded as though he was badly hurt.

Mealie Jimmy heard the sound of the bullet and the scream before he got to the car. The correct procedure was to radio in, then go and help Deckham. The knighthood was almost there. Then he saw the crouching figure and saw the weapon. Deckham would be finished if he left him. Mealie Jimmy turned back, moving slowly and ponderously. He hadn't been seen yet and he watched the rifle go up into the shoulder and heard Deckham opening up the night with his bloody yelling.

'All right. That'll be enough of that.'

He'd used the words a thousand times before. As a constable, as a sergeant and as an inspector. After that he'd been too big and too grand to handle the bully boys in person. But it never failed. There was always the hesitation, the moment of doubt in face of an implacable advance. He saw the figure stiffen and the gun come up. Keep going, no faster, no slower. Cow them with the sheer bloody majesty of the Law. And here was his fucking majesty on the receiving end of a bloody gun. Well, it wasn't the first time. That was what had started it all – the long bloody rise and now just once more and there was a knighthood round the corner. But knighthood or no knighthood, he wished he'd brought a gun.

He was no more than three yards away. He saw the face for the first time. A girl! Bloody hell. How would this one move? Keep going.

'Now, miss. Don't be a fool. Just let me have that gun.'

She let him have it all right. Two bloody blasts from the hip. Mealie Jimmy felt the lead tear at his flesh. He staggered slightly, then came on again.

'Now that wasn't clever, miss. Be sensible, just give me the gun. There's a good girl.'

The next shot took him in the chest and still he came on. Zircon Two stared in disbelief. She knew she had hit him each time. She panicked and fired wildly, turning to run. She didn't see the great form of Mealie Jimmy lean forward and slowly topple over on to the lawn. There'd be no knighthood now. Only the plain gun-metal cross on its plain blue ribbon and that they'd give to his widow. Deckham started to vomit his relief.

·   ·   ·   ·   ·

The sergeant of River Police looked curiously at Rigbey as they dropped down the river. The man just stood in the cockpit and stared ahead. Hadn't said a word since they had cast off.

They slipped under Westminster Bridge and Rigbey spoke for the first time.

'Lights out.'

The helmsman switched off the boat's lights.

'Throttle right back, let the tide take you.'

The boat slowed and the engine beat became almost imperceptible, only just giving steerage way. They came gently down to Hungerford Bridge, barely moving with the tide. Rigbey held up his good hand.

'Drop below the bridge, then turn and come up to each pile in turn.'

The sergeant nodded. The tide was on the turn and they were almost at slack water. He stood by with a boat hook. So this was it, was it? By Gaw! It would make a right mess if that lot went up.

Rigbey searched each pile in turn, more and more puzzled at finding nothing. It had to be here. They had talked freely in the Fulham house and this must be the place. Desperately he groped below the sluggish water.

Nothing again – but it was an idea – try them all again. Slowly the boat moved from massive column to massive column. He found it on the fourth try – a great bolster of waterproofed explosive with a shaped exterior held at barely negative buoyancy so that it would float just below the level of the water.

The Belgians had worked hurriedly but had done a good job. Quarter-inch flexible stainless-steel wire rope held the explosives in position. Helped by the sergeant he tore and worried at the wire with the boat's tools and finally parted it.

'Grab it, man. Don't let it go!' There was a rumble overhead and the whole bridge shook as an early train went over. It was still dark but the commuters were beginning to pour into the city.

The sergeant caught the floating bundle with the boat hook.

'Now hold it with us!'

The sergeant leaned out and his hand slipped. He made a wild grab but the bundle bobbed out of reach floating gently away.

'It's gone, sir.'

'No matter. We'll get after it when we've checked the other piles. If there's anything more it will be on the next one.'

Rigbey was right. Another thick pad of waterproofed explosive. He started to work on the wire when a searchlight stabbed out from downstream. That would be them – the Wolves. The light left them and flickered over the other piles, checking for any other opposition. Rigbey abandoned his work on the wire and searched frantically for the lead to the detonators – the wire that must run back to the boat – the wire that would carry the electric charge that would set off the explosive. First find the explosive, then take the boat. There he would kill the leader of the Wolves.

.　　.　　.　　.　　.

On the cabin cruiser Fafner stared in disbelief. The Zircons had come tumbling aboard a quarter of an hour before with their tales of surprise and successful escape. There was only twenty minutes to go before there would be two of the early-morning trains halted on the bridge. Then would be the time. But now the searchlight had confirmed the look-out's alarm and there were men working where the explosives should be. Fafner stared at Agate One. He was taking over command.

'It will have to be at the next train. We must explode then.'

From the riverside there were two winks of light from an orange shaded torch that told of a train approaching. They saw its lights come up over the South Bank. Fafner nodded to Agate One.

'Now!'

Agate One pulled down on the switch that would set off the two great charges three hundred yards upstream. As he pulled at the switch he saw the unnatural angle of one of the plastic-covered wires that connected the switch to the charges. One of them was hanging slack, almost at right angles to the switchboard, instead of pointing ahead, straight over the bows. The warning sprang to his brain, even as his hand was moving on the switch, but it was too late to stop. The whole river erupted by the side of the cruiser, lifting it up and breaking it apart in an eye-bursting blast of explosive. The planks bulged out then tore into fragments and the glass from the cabin shattered into a thousand missiles.

It was a metal cleat, torn from the splintered decking, that killed Fafner. It struck him on the side of the head, smashing it to bloody pulp. Agate One and most of the Belgians died too. Only the girl, Zircon Two, survived. The explosive which Rigbey had released from the bridge had been carried by the slow-moving water, guided by the tiny pull of the plastic lead, to no more than six feet from the cruiser when it went up.

Rigbey threw himself back into the wildly rocking patrol boat clutching the severed end of the second lead. He held on to the cockpit rail and watched the pieces of wreckage dropping slowly back into the water through the orange blaze of fuel. He felt only despair. Too late – too late once more to kill.

He turned to the patrolmen. Their faces, shocked by the explosion, were incongruously ruddy in the light from the flames. They stared at him. The sergeant spoke first.

'What do we do now, sir?'

Rigbey looked again over the destruction, then turned away.

'Nothing,' he said. 'There is nothing more to do.'

Epilogue

The man with the black glove on his left hand sipped his glass of wine. It was lunchtime and he was in one of the greatest of the many great restaurants of Paris.

He saw the heads of the other people turning as she came in and he sat back to watch the familiar spectacle.

She insisted on spending her own money on her clothes and she was dressed exquisitely, a flowing silk that glowed and caught the light and shone with subdued colours. She was some way down the long aisle that divided the tables before people really noticed her.

He glanced to his left. The people there could see only the right side of her face and he saw the looks of interest from the men, the ogling from the elderly and the darting appraising glances from the women. On the other side of the room it was different: distaste from the squeamish, the quick embarrassed return to eating – eyes firmly on the plate, from the merely polite and the concern and pity from the kind at heart.

Then he was standing and she was with him and the aura of her perfume was around him. As she sat she reached out and squeezed his fingers through the glove. Always the left hand where the flesh barely covered the bones.

She smiled. The pout was still there, the slight thrusting forward of the lips until it reached the left side of her face when it disappeared into the desert of shiny scar tissue and the awful cavity under the eye where the cheek-bone had once been. And the eye itself – the eye that could not see, moving, but without life.

James Rigbey covered her hand with his good fingers.

'Welcome, my lovely.' As always he saw the tears that began to shine and she blew a kiss across the table, then began to search her handbag.

'James. Great excitement. Tassie and Mark want to come and stay at the farm. A whole fortnight, if we'll have them. Now why do you think they want to do . . . ?'

181

Rigbey smiled. 'I know, my darling. Mark told me. He's thinking of taming that Hardwicke girl and turning her into a domestic drudge and he wants to observe marital bliss at first hand. We're having an inundation from Security, aren't we? Sarah and the Fafner kids last week and now the heavies.'

Juliette's eyes softened. 'Darling, aren't the Fafner children growing up well. To think what their parents were like and to see them . . . Well, heredity can't be that important, can it?'

Rigbey smiled. 'It's the church background. When the archdeacon decided to adopt them I wondered if he wasn't taking on too much but when you see Sarah's mum, happy as a cat with kittens . . .' He broke off and started to laugh. 'I've just thought. At law those two must be Sarah's brother and sister now.'

The *maître* moved up to their table. Over the past year they had become favoured clients.

'Ah! Mme Rigbey, how nice to see you again.' Very professional, but the kiss to hand had a warmth to it that other diners rarely got. They became lost in the menu for a moment then, when it was dealt with . . .

'But, James, about Tassie and Mark. I was going to give them separate rooms, do you think I . . . ?'

Rigbey smiled. He seemed to be always smiling these days. 'Just do that, my darling. Mark can find his way in the dark.' He saw the questioning, doubting look, wary of being teased. He reached out and patted her hand. 'Truly, my darling, it will do them good. Just keep them well away from our part. Julia's wonderful but a howling three-month-old kid can put any lusty male off the idea of marriage.'

She was relieved, but there was something else. Something else at the back of her mind. She took a deep breath and it came out in a rush.

'Darling, I know we said we would never talk about the past. But . . . well . . .' She started to fiddle with her napkin, eyes on her plate. 'Well, darling, Tassie asked if she could see Cerise Nolan while she's over here, as she's so close.' She went on hurriedly, anxious not to be misunderstood. 'Darling, of course she can come but I thought – well!' She gave an embarrassed shrug. 'Well, they said you'd hurt her – to make her tell things.'

She looked up at him apologetically asking for forgiveness.

Rigbey smiled ruefully.

'My darling, I didn't touch her.'

She was puzzled.

'But there were burns on her thumb. They said from a light socket. Isn't that why you had to leave Security?'

Rigbey silently cursed the loud mouth who had blabbed the cover story.

He looked into his wife's eyes.

'Just dabs from a cigarette end – purely for show. We had to satisfy her bosses that she'd held out almost to the end. She was a good girl – after I had shown her . . . well . . . shown her something.'

He saw the relief in her eyes and she sat back in her chair, anxious to change the subject.

'What do you think of this?' She held out her arms so that the silk showed its colours.

'Beautiful, my darling. You must be the best-dressed wife of a French farmer above the butter line. And as for what's underneath!' He reached his hand out under the table and touched her knee. He felt the answering pressure. He looked around the room at the bored faces, the petulance and the indifference – he whispered.

'I think I'm probably unique among the men in this room.'

'Why, darling?'

He gripped her knee tightly.

'Because I'm in love with my wife.'